AN EX'

KNOT

A Different World War

(PART V)

HUGH LUPUS

APS BOOKS

APS Publications,
4 Oakleigh Road,
Stourbridge,
West Midlands,
DY8 2JX

APS Books is a subsidiary of the APS Publications imprint

www.andrewsparke.com

First published worldwide by APS Books in 2020

A catalogue record for this book is available from the British Library

Stuka cover photograph courtesy of Bundesarchiv Bild 183-J16050/CC-BY-SA 3.0

ISBN 978-1-78996-148-5

AN EXTRA KNOT PART V

SISTERS, DAUGHTERS, WIVES AND MOTHERS

Up, and roll far.

Down, and roll far.

Up and down.

Roll and roll.

Wave after steep wave.

Skid a little at the top as propeller churns air and rudder fights for bite.

Over and over.

Slow, but with resolve uncommon.

Over and over was the Bittersweet's life.

A corvette's life.

A guardian's life.

Hank Reaver's life.

To send the probing sound down and out into the waves.

Over and over.

Through bright blue days or grey locked skies

Over and over.

Through nights where the stars wheeled or nights where black wave and black heaven met.

Over and over.

With resolve uncommon.

With skin that never warmed, never dried.

With eyes that saw with sweat blurring.

With ears that heard with caution warning.

A guardian's life.

An uncommon life.

Hank's life.

A corvette's life.

She felt the fingers touch her, long before she saw their owners.

Delicate fingers with held back power.

The radar chattered to itself and then hurried back to its owner.

'What ship?' The Destroyer's voice was curt, not unfriendly but shaded by stern duty. 'Where bound?'

There was a custom which bound them both now and she was determined to follow it lest her challenger thought ill of her.

'I am the Bittersweet, four days out from the new found land and bound for Belfast docks. I guard my charges as is my right, who are you that would ask these things?'

The Destroyer was about to answer when a different voice was heard. This voice was a warm contralto interwoven with braids of cold steel, despite its warmth it was a voice that commanded, that would brook no dispute.

'You lay your cartel well sister. Truly I have never heard better. You do yourself much honour. Forgive my escort. They too have duties, and those duties are to carry me to a safe berth where my hurts may be healed.'

A wave lifted her then and she got a brief glimpse of a huge ship, much stained by war. Flame had run down her side leaving old soot and fresh rust, one of her main guns lay forlornly down as if resting after long exertion and a thousand small wounds were scattered along her body.

A wave, cousin to the one which was sending her skywards attempted to challenge the huge ship, but a sharp bow cut the wave, plunging down into the wetness and scattering it into spume and salt-licked rainbows.

'You are hurt!'

There was pride in the reply. 'A little, but my wounds were bought in honourable combat and are but a small price to pay for victory. Our enemies in the middle sea are no more, now I may rest for a short time before I place myself in the lists once again.'

An image of flame rent night, of screams and thunder came to her and for a moment she wished that she could be a mighty warship instead of a mere caretaker.

'I wish I could have been there.' There was a little resentment in the Bittersweet's answer, for in truth her duties were plain enough and there was little chance for advancement in her life, but the huge ships answer was surprisingly gentle.

'I wish you could have been there also, sister, for your spirit is such as I would wish to see in any who bear my flag, yet I would charge you not to scorn that with which you have been entrusted. If I have had the honour of destroying those who would stand against me, then you have the honour of protection, and who shall say which is the greater honour?

'To win in battle is one thing, but to walk lonely ramparts without respite is a duty hard, an uncommon task for uncommon sisters.

'And think you this; what use my vaunted speed if my hearts beat no more for lack of fuel, what then of my mighty guns if my powder rooms ache from hunger?

'No, if I and my sisters have been bright swords, then you and yours have been a hard shield and of what use is the one without the other?

'Walk your lonely path little sister, walk it with honour bright as you do now.'

And with that the voice ended. The next high wave gave only a glimpse of smoke upon the horizon.

There was only up and down now for Hank Reaver and the Bittersweet.

Up

And roll far.

Down.

And roll far.

Over and over.

Slow.

But with resolve.

Uncommon resolve.

Down.

Cut through waves green and white.

Up.

Say farewell to the convoy eastward bound.

Down.

Say farewell to the little corvette brave and true.

Head towards a setting sun and a haven.

Up.

Down.

The same rhythm, the dance decades old.

The convoy a salt-tinged smudge on a far horizon.

Time for last words and true words.

Praise for the guarding of flocks made an honour brighter yet.

On and on through the waters green and white, while rust red and brown stained her sides and a tired crew tended her with love.

Hard pressed she had been but war skill had seen her triumph.

An enemy put to the sword and the middle sea itself set aflame.

A night and a day had witnessed sweet victory.

But at a cost.

Her children were safe, cosseted and wrapped well against the sea's careless malevolence but she bore scars as well as rust and worst of all she grieved. A last fiery shell had sought admittance to a turret whose guns had pointed towards an enemy horizon and armour had sternly done all it could.

And failed.

She felt the fireball as a sharp pain even as cries of victory were heard from all around.

Three turrets fired revenge in angry salvoes and then smaller sisters gathered round her victim and pushed hot spears into her burning sides until the sea took her.

It was over then and the morning battle about to begin and she still had sisters to command.

But later and in the days that followed she grieved as flag-draped men took a final voyage.

She wept salt tears as they fell and watched them take a last bed.

She bade them a final adieu and promised that never would they be forgotten.

On and on, the next wave and the next.

Grieving and tired of war, the cost of honour and duty, the loss of friends.

On and on, one sun birthing the next until at a twilight's last flaring a voice came from the gathering gloom challenging those who sought to cross a border. Stern challenge changed to warm welcome as she made her presence known. Tugs, squat and greasy added their power to engines long over used and pushed and prodded her graceful bulk into a friendly berth.

And then it was over.

Long months of command, of sea miles uncounted, of battle red and raw was over.

The Hood was back to an old home...yet new.

The Hood was back in Boston.

Back with old friends...and new.

Back to have her wounds tended...and better.

But most of all to rest.

And that was best of all.

SAFE HARBOUR

The engine room telegraph bell rang and the pointer moved to a welcome sight and Stebbings muttered a prayer that thanked an unseen deity with a mix of gratitude and blasphemy.

'Finished with engines!' He turned to a weary crew and spoke with his best petty officer's voice.

'Well what are you waiting for, an engraved invitation? Valves and brakes and be quick about it or you lot will feel the toe of my boot!'

His crew grinned for they were a good crew and needed little in the way of orders after such a long cruise.

There was an art to shutting down an engine even as there was an art to starting one. Steam had to be bled off slowly to match a diminishing fuel, great asbestos lined brakes must be placed against spinning shafts lest inertia overcome care and all these acts must be balanced the one with the other in a dance where a single misstep would bring hurt and torn metal.

He could leave his crew to carry on for they were comrades to be trusted and he walked over to where a thin man in a stained white overall was standing next to the great box of the main centre shaft bearing.

The bearing still carried its load but cried softly as it did so, somewhere inside hard chromium had been lost and now dull steel pushed against the slowing shaft. Only hourly applications of grease had averted a greater calamity and Stebbings watched as the man gently stroked the casing as a man would calm a loved horse that had been over-ridden.

'Finished with engines, sir, the lads are shutting down now.'

The man lifted his hand from the casing and turned.

'Thank you, Mr. Stebbings, nothing more to report?'

'No sir, spares and defect list is on your desk ready to sign…it's a long list; us and the Yanks are going to be busy for a while I think.'

Pulver gave a sad smile. 'We drove the old girl hard didn't we, but she never let us down, never refused us, never gave us anything but her best. But she's tired, just listen to her.'

The sobbing of the bearing was just a single voice in a sad chorus; steam whistled through joints that begged for repair, generators crackled through coils that trembled on the edge of breakdown and everywhere the damage inflicted by the recoil of the Hood's great guns grunted in barely mastered pain.

'She deserves a rest and that's God's own truth.'

Stebbings nodded his understanding and laid his own arm on a trembling stanchion.

'But a bit of leave sir and that can't be bad; few days maybe and then back into it. We'll soon get the old girl back on her feet, us and the Yanks between us.'

Pulver shook his head. 'No, Patrick, not for us. For others maybe, but not for us.' He pulled out a grease stained paper and a small envelope from an overall pocket. 'Orders, Patrick, orders. There will be leave, but it will be home leave. We're going home, Pat, home at last.'

Pulver was smiling now thinking of grey-green eyes and a child never met while Stebbings stood with a mouth half open and thoughts of Doris and the kids running through a mind which barely grasped the idea.

'Home?'

'Home, Pat, were going home. There'll be leave and then we have a job to do together. But leave first, see the family.' He paused and then thrust the envelope into Stebbings' hand. 'Congratulations Pat, you did the work and you more than deserve this.'

Stebbings opened the envelope to find a cloth badge embroidered with a crown and gold oak leaves.

'Well done, Chief Petty Officer.'

He'd been promoted and that was something, but more, much more than that he was going home.

Home, he was going home.

And that was best of all.

The last oil-fed flame flickered and died, the last ounce of steam fled into the condensers and a great peace settled onto the Hood. One by one she bade her parts rest and promised to reawaken them when time and duty called. There was little to do now but wait and endure the touch of men who sought to heal with hammer, torch and wrench.

She felt wooden fingers reach out and run over her wounds and a familiar voice sound from a nearby wharf.

'You look a mite banged up, child but you're in good hands now. Best you rest up some and let my people work.' There was an oaken chuckle from the Constitution. 'I've had a touch of that myself over the years and I ain't the ship I was and that's for sure. Why there ain't a part of me from keel to main top that's original but I'm still the same old girl that I was.

'Now tell me about the war, I've been bustin' my britches waiting to hear all about it so best you settle down and sit for a spell and start talking. How did my daughters do? I'd have given my copper bottom to be there.'

The Hood began to talk, praising the American ships, stressing their ability to quickly learn from those who had long wielded sharp knives.

She told of small ships guided by great men, though young. Ships that thrust and parried, weakening the enemy by day and by night, while larger sisters learnt and relearnt until lessons were instincts honed to cutting blades.

She told of a slow war, breaking enemy pathways one by one, killing ships one by one, two by two, until the enemy stung by repeated challenge sallied out in a single battle that began in the dark of night and ended under a morning's sun.

The Hood said little about her actions for a warrior gave no heed to idle boasting but she told of the Texas and sisters many who stood and slammed a door shut with shot and shell and how the night was split with fire and death.

She told of how the Dunkerque had sailed with her one last time and given her absolution before the Black wave had lifted her with gentle arms.

The Constitution said little during the Hood's words not wishing to break the flow, but building up a picture of war and battle, but finally as the words came to an end, she spoke with a voice that trembled with joy. 'A night action and my daughters in the thick of it! Child you have no idea how that warms me, all my lessons have been well heeded and you guided them with skill but the old flag still flies high and not a speck of dishonour lies on it.'

The Hood chuckled at a memory. 'In truth their only sin was a light one and one easily corrected. They held fast to your command to let no day pass without an enemy hurt and held fast all too well, but stern words taught that the sure kill is ever the best kill.

'They took your flag into war and though it was torn by battle it flew high and flies high yet. When you and your daughters meet, shower them with praise for few deserve it better.'

'And you saw the black wave', said the Constitution, 'saw it myself off Valparaiso back in '39. Course I was a young shaveling back then and not used to seeing such things. But I saw one o' them little trading brigs decide she weren't goin' to do her work no more and split herself in two, now this was deliberate mind, and no accident. It was plain orneriness and no mistake. Well the Black Wave came up and gripped that little brig like a terrier grips a rat and my how that brig squealed! But it weren't no use, the Black Wave took her and I don't want to think no more about it. The Black Wave punishes lack of duty and that's no error, but you do your duty and the wave is like a little lamb.

'I guess your friend found that out and to my mind she's in a better place. She did her duty and then some, ain't no cause to worry about her no more. Few beat the wave and it comes for us all either early or late and we all owe it a death. But duty, child, duty is the light that guides us and don't you forget it.

'Can the merchantman fight? Can the oiler ward the wolves by running? Is the liner to place her masts against the pirate? As once they looked to me, now they look to you and my daughters, for as the oiler and the merchantman have their duties so we that have teeth have ours.'

The Hood thought of her dead, of mangled limbs and red, red blood scattered and splashed. There were voices now that could speak only through her and her sadness fell away for the dead were sad enough and it was for the living to remember.

Her crew and every part of her had never asked for guarantees, that much she knew. All who bore the flag and wore the uniform risked the same fate, all had faced the same choice and all who bore the flag and wore the uniform had made the same decision.

They would fight for home harbours and home firesides, for sisters and comrades, for kith and for kin.

They would fight to preserve the familiar and the good, fight for well-trodden streets, the church and the chapel.

They would fight not out of desire but out of obligation to serve those who could not fight, whose only weapon was prayer.

To die was to die with sadness, but with honour bright.

The Constitution's words were comforting and the light of duty flared high within her once more.

Yet the war was a thing that would not die. The Black Wave was overworked and the conversation turned from war past to war yet to come. It was a conversation that the Hood knew would raise memories still green, yet what she must say could not be delayed and the traditions of the service dictated that sooner begun was sooner finished.

She shifted a little in her berth and began. 'When my hurts are healed, when I am new fashioned once more, I do not return to the narrow seas nor yet the inland sea that is ours once more. My course lies otherwise, I will travel to the father of all seas, for there dwell the enemies who wear the rising sun. There I will lead a great war band, trusted warriors all and help clear the waters that lie under Capricorn's gaze.'

There was a silence from the Constitution at these words for there was still anger and grief at daughters murdered by treachery and dishonour. The old ship had very definite ideas of what was right and what was wrong and the deaths of daughters caught at peaceful anchor had burnt within her a bitter sense of outrage.

At last a voice darker than midnight floated across from the Constitution's wharf. 'Child, in the great water I have many daughters and each to each I have given a special order. To that flag there is to be given no mercy, no accepting of honourable surrender, no terms save that of death. Each daughter, both old and new has taken this vow and I ask now what is your mind in this matter.'

The old ship had asked a question and asked it in the old way, formal and courteous. There was an answer to give but it must be given with the right words and in the proper manner, for, friendship apart, the iron oak timbers held a voice which deserved respect.

'Long ago', the Hood replied, 'I too took a vow before you. I vowed that your fight was my fight, that your daughters were in very truth my sisters. I do not make vows in vain. I made the oath and I am bound by its words. From me the flag of the rising sun will take no ruth. From me and from mine there will be no grace and no forgiveness.

'Even now my host gathers, even now they gather in strength and in numbers and when the day comes as come it must my host will exact vengeance for murdered daughters.'

'This is my pledge, mine and my sisters, these are my words, mine and my host.'

It was done, the words had been spoken, the vow rebirthed and once more there was a silence from the Constitution until the dark voice was replaced was replaced by one more familiar.

'Asked and answered, though I never doubted the answer, still it is good to hear the words. I've sailed the great waters before and there's no waters like them; at night the stars meet the waves and at day the sky is blue and blue with nary a cloud to be seen. Go south and the wind is fit to blow the sticks out of you and even the albatrosses flee, too far north and fogs as thick as pea soup grip every rope and spar.'

There was a wistful sigh.

'I sure wish I could see those waves again and feel the salt wind in my sails.'

'Your place is here', replied the Hood softly. 'Where else are daughters to learn all that is gentle except at your knee? And I too must learn, for the waters of the Great Father are too little known to me. There are currents there and winds that are greatly to be feared, tell me all that you know, that I may better lead my host.'

A soft chuckle bounced from wharf to wharf.

'I reckon you've come to the right place to learn, child, so settle while I tell a few tales. Now there's a place off the Sea of Japan where cold water bumps up against warm and the winds that come from that are something to behold. Now the best thing to be done is this...'

All through the Boston night the Constitution gave cautions and warnings; places where the wind died to a whisper or blew with full throated rage, the dead places where the waves were feeble and the seaweed danced in stately time under a hot sun that was a dread to men and timbers alike.

All this and more as the ship's bells announced the waning of the dark and the advancing of the light.

And in the morning the first workman walked aboard the Hood and the first cutting torch flared into bright healing warmth.

American skill would refit her for her war to come.

And that was better yet.

EIGHT WEEKS

They'd been given eight weeks and not a second more.

Eight weeks to reform and re-fashion.

Eight weeks, and at the end of that time everything must be in place and ready.

Eight weeks for the men of Jarrow to work an old magic, practice an old skill.

Eight weeks did not frighten Geordie McIntyre but the bridge of the Dithmarschen did. Even the Navy acknowledged that it really had been an extraordinary lucky shot. The destroyer's shell had hit and then burst in a savage blossoming that had scoured Captain, helmsman and everyone on the bridge from life.

Geordie McIntyre shuddered at what he was seeing.

Great rents, fanged with sharp steel were everywhere and every tube and instrument were smashed beyond repair while the telegraph reminded him of a broken tooth pulled by an inept dentist.

It would have been quick he thought, *the destroyer looming out of the fog, a moment of panic and then nothing.*

A boarding party had scrambled aboard before the blood had stopped dripping and the Dithmarschen had changed ownership and sailed to Jarrow under control of a prize crew.

Despite the damage Geordie was most impressed with the ship. She was fast at twenty-three knots and well-built for the Germans were fine craftsmen and there was very little she could not do from pumping fuel to mending broken legs. The apparatus and supplies for the mending of legs was not why the Dithmarschen had been sent to Jarrow though. Someone had seen something on the ship which was very interesting and decided to let the men of Palmers shipyards run expert eyes over it.

A long week had been given to survey her and Geordie had consulted far and wide. He now had a long list of suggestions. Secretly he was proud of the list for it represented a good deal of hard work and a change in how the ship yards were run. The shipyard was a far different place today and though he was too modest to say so Geordie was responsible for a good deal of that.

Everyone respected the man who had walked from Jarrow to London and forced a government to give work to starving families.

An argument between union and management died when Geordie arrived, disputes over demarcation, over payments or work hours faded away before a prestige he had never sought.

Always he listened trying to find a path both could agree on and a decision made by him was rarely challenged for he was a court of last appeal. Yet he bore the weight with calm good sense, a ready smile and no sense of arrogance for he was a man born with no sense of self-importance.

Eight weeks.

Eight weeks to convert engines, to rip and to gut.

There were those who disbelieved. 'You can do all this in eight weeks?'

Geordie did not know the man, nor did the man know Palmers so his pride was only hurt a little. 'Why man, if it wasn't fo' the diesels we wud hev it done in five, and divvent yee doubt it!'

The man in the suit had returned to London only half believing.

Eight weeks.

Geordie smiled as the first red arms of the sun hit the grey wet waves of the Tyne.

He smiled as the first of the men and boys walked up to the ship and his voice laughed down at them. 'Hey canny lads wot are yee waitin' fo'? There's wark hor, are yee ready?'

A chorus of good-humoured insults floated up through the chill morning air and soon the first hammer made the first blow.

Eight weeks for the Dithmarschen and the men of Jarrow

Eight weeks.

Newly promoted or not Chief Petty Officer Patrick Stebbings was frightened.

Admirals were creatures best avoided, best left alone and never ever approached. Not to be in the same room as one would be something he would willingly give a month's rum ration for or perhaps it was a situation better faced with a month's rum ration safe inside him, but

14

here he was in an office in London facing a Rear Admiral who was looking at them with what Stebbings hoped was a benign expression.

Of course, Lieutenant Pulver was here, like him dressed in his number one uniform, but unlike him seemingly unaffected by the presence of exalted rank.

'Sit down gentlemen and make yourselves comfortable. You are no doubt wondering why you have been summoned here. Well there are several reasons the first and most important one is this ship.'

He rose and handed the two men a photograph of a workmanlike ship equipped with derricks and booms.

'The Dithmarschen is a German supply boat. The Relentless caught her off the coast of France, boarded her and brought her back almost intact. Quite a nice piece of work in my opinion. However, the Dithmarschen is a rather unusual ship, the Germans are feeling the pinch regarding their U-boat campaign; The Asturians harry them as they leave France, we have our bases here and, on the Azores, while the Americans press down from Iceland. All in all, it's not a happy time for the Kreigsmarine, but once in the Atlantic a U-boat has a fair degree of safety, but on its return journey it has once more to run the gauntlet. The Germans realised this and have adapted ships like the Dithmarschen to a new purpose. Far better in their mind for the U-boat itself to remain on station while these ships slip out from France with new crews and fresh fuel and equipment, and then make their way back to France.

'Naturally we have our own thoughts on this and the Relentless was one of a number of ships tasked with ensuring that this particular plan was frustrated. I cannot go into details, but it seems that many U-boat crews will miss their rendezvous. Rather a bad business for them but how they manage their affairs is no concern of mine or yours either. Now, having studied the photographs, what is the first thing you gentlemen have noticed?'

He looked quizzically at the men and awaited an answer.

Stebbings looked at Pulver and pointed to a spot on the photograph.

Pulver nodded and spoke. 'The refueling booms, sir. They are midships and not aft.'

The admiral looked pleased and grinned.

'Exactly so. In theory the Dithmarschen can replenish two U-boat at the same time, though we don't know if that has ever been attempted. It is though something we intend to undertake and you two gentlemen will be part of that experiment.

'We are sending a fleet to the Pacific; the distances are huge and our bases few and far apart. Our old methods of replenishing at sea are to say the least cumbersome and wholly unfitted for such a campaign. We must therefore take a leaf out of the American song book and change our tactics.

'I'm sending you to see the Dithmarschen undertake sea trials and exercises. I will expect a full report with recommendations and I want that report rather sooner than later.'

This was a direct order and could only be obeyed, but a small devil of doubt appeared in Stebbings' soul. It grew and grew until it was strong enough to kill his fear of admirals and strong enough to force the words from his throat.

'Excuse me sir, but why us?'

The devil laughed and retreated with Stebbings astonished at his own boldness.

To his surprise the admiral did not blast him with molten fire and reduce him several stages in rank. Instead he began to tick off points on his fingers.

'Firstly, because you were recommended. Secondly because your ship is laid up in Boston and you can be spared. Thirdly because the Dithmarschen is joining the Royal Auxiliary Fleet under the name *Susannah*, now does that give you a clue?'

Stebbings looked blankly at the smiling face of the admiral. He was obviously supposed to see what the name had to do with both of them, but no matter how hard he thought he could not make the connection and it was Pulver who came to the rescue.

'Susannah was the wife of the first Lord Hood, sir. Are you suggesting…?'

'I'm not suggesting anything, Lieutenant. The Hood and her escorts will need a fast ship to aid them…a wife if you will. The Susannah will be that ship…if you recommend her to be so. Your orders are with my staff, go to Jarrow and report back as soon as possible.'

And so it was that Stebbings and Pulver found themselves on the express train that ran arrow-straight up to the border lands watered by the mighty River Tyne.

SUSANNAH

'If you do that again I...I will bite you; you see if I don't!'

The voice was angry and belonged to the Bacchante which was now festooned with angry fluttering flags and an Aldis light which stuttered its displeasure in a series barking flashes.

The reply was not long in coming and was not at all angry but held definite tones of mocking laughter. 'Not so easy is it? You think you rule the sea, but I say you are amateurs unfit to sail with one such as I!'

This was the voice of the Dithmarschen who now sailed under the name Susannah and there was nothing pleasant or feminine in the voice, and the mocking laughter continued. 'Amateur!'

There was a low growl from the Bacchante who spoke from gritted teeth. 'We...will...try...that...again. And for heaven's sake keep still this time!'

Andrew Stebbings, newly promoted Chief Petty officer could swear fluently in several languages none of which seemed adequate to express the frustration he felt.

He winced again as the Bacchante and the Susannah met beam to beam in a great rush, and for the third time this morning the Navy ship's Aldis light signaled its displeasure.

It would be ironic, he thought *to be killed within sight of land after surviving several hazardous battles and more than a few bar fights by a ship that technically bore him no ill will at all.*

The problem was well known of course; two or more ships travelling close together at speed in the same direction did something to the water between them which caused each ship to become far too attracted to each other with loud and potentially dangerous collisions the result.

Mr. Pulver had attempted to explain just what was happening, something to do with water pressure or the lack of it, but all he knew was that there was a fine line between too slow and too fast and even the slightest difference in heading was enough to cause yet another collision.

The Bacchante had swung round in an angry curve and Stebbings watched her crew rearrange the collection of nets and mats which were supposed to lessen the impact of several thousand tons of steel colliding with another several thousand tons of steel.

He hoped that this would work, he most sincerely hoped.

Because the Bacchante was getting bigger and closer.

Fast.

'Keep still you little bastard, keep still and let me come alongside…and no tricks this time!'

Again, there was the sneering reply which sought to anger and distress the Bacchante.

'No tricks are needed, enemy. Your own stupidity will prove that you are unfitted for even such a simple task as this. I am the better ship and it is time to admit that you are defeated.'

There was no answer from the Bacchante only a questing bow that began to overlap the stern of the Susannah.

And the game began once more.

There was a mathematical formula which ruled the approach of the two ships and Pulver had factored in everything that could possibly influence it; displacement, speed, wind and the exact shape that each ship imprinted on the water. Each one had been given due weight and the neat figures on pristine white paper did not lie.

Except they did.

There were too many variables; wave action, the exact degree that the engine gauges misread, even the small amount each ships compass was in error. All this and much more made a mockery of his perfect mathematics and he had long since recognised that his neat penmanship could never be more than a sign post that pointed in the right direction. But Pulver was a very small part of a very large force which had a long tradition of failing to recognise the word *impossible* and so where mathematics had failed skill would come to the rescue. The new method of replenishment at sea would be learnt not through scribbles on a page but through hard work and much bitter experience.

And notes, many, many notes. Pulver's note book no longer bore precise mathematical symbols but hastily scribbled thoughts that would reduce the geometry of chance and half hidden laws into a wisdom that reacted to a capricious wind and sea with a fine-tuned skill that could be taught to others.

He heard the helmsman acknowledge his orders and watched the Susannah grow ever nearer, watched her wake grow ever whiter. Perhaps this time frustration would be relieved, perhaps this time success would come their way.

He could only hope.

Because the stern of the Susannah was looming up.

Fast.

'You bastard, you did that on purpose!'

At the last second an errant wave pushed the stern of the Susannah a few yards nearer the Bacchante and in an instant the water between them became subtly lighter and only frantic maneuvering averted another collision.

Every part of her complained in a chorus which only spurred her anger.

'On purpose, and don't tell me that it was an accident. I should load and fire, teach you a little manners!'

'But you won't', the reply still held contempt and no little scorn, 'because if you do it will show that I was the better ship. I am a captive, a slave, I do as I am bid and only as I am bid. The fault is yours and only yours. Now do you wish to try again or shall you return to port with the stench of failure hanging over you?'

A long howl of frustration came from the Bacchante and angry propellers churned the water in a Curving, bubbling wake.

'We…will…try…again.'

And the game continued.

The bridge of the Susannah had not been a happy place that afternoon, nor was it any happier in the days that followed.

Each day the Bacchante and the Susannah danced in the deep waters and each day tempers grew shorter even as the sun stayed longer in the heavens.

But even the brightest sun must fade and todays sun had begun its descent long hours past and both Stebbings and Pulver stood on the foredeck of the Bacchante watching the heavens with mounting dread.

A black lowering sky and restless wind that teased and harried the waves were all signs that both men recognised. There would be time for just one more trial before Father Tempest roared his displeasure and forced the ships to run towards sheltering land.

Pulver glanced up to a rain-splattered bridge and the pale faces that lived within it. Much depended on those faces for the for the Susannah was the first of many ships which must be become floating havens in the vast blue Pacific.

It must be so, but so far success had run through their fingers like fairy gold and even Stebbings who was at heart an optimist was looking decidedly gloomy.

'Just time for one more go, sir, then we best make a run for it I reckon.'

Pulver nodded, his eyes not fixed upon the growing bulk of the Susannah but remaining locked on the bridge as if by sheer willpower he could guarantee success.

The stern of the Bacchante lifted, plunging the bow of the destroyer into a green wave which gave wet greeting to both men who ignored such minor inconveniences as sailors have ever done.

The wave was but a herald of the storm to come and the wind rose yet more, whistling its malice, teasing the waves into anger and still the two ships grew closer and closer.

Stebbings shrugged, the water streaming off his oilskins and joining the remnants of previous incursions. 'Here we go again, fingers crossed!'

And for the last time on a dark afternoon the dance began.

'Again? Have the last weeks taught you nothing, enemy? Have you not learnt that you are not my equal in this sea or any other?' The voice of the Susannah was decidedly male, decidedly German and decidedly sarcastic and it was a voice the Bacchante was decidedly tired of hearing so she did not reply. There was no conversation between them now only a mutual and dogged determination to triumph over the other.

The Susannah held her speed and her heading as much as wild wind and frantic wave would allow while the cautious screws of the Bacchante edged her closer to a hated adversary.

A wave more feral than most pushes her with evil fingers and she lurches towards the Susannah, but a helmsman now more practiced does not wait for orders and gives the slightest turn of helm and the wave is thwarted in an explosion of angry spume and spray that is rightly ignored.

Slower and watchful the two ships draw nearer yet. The wind seeing his servant waves defeated, howls his displeasure and tries by main strength to push the two ships together and add to the collection of dents and gouges that both ships sport.

He in turn is defeated and twists his powers to the darkening clouds, turning them ever blacker and ever lower to a white whipped sea.

'We…will…try…again.'

The voice of the Bacchante could hardly be heard over the crash of the waves and the gasping lungs of an angry Father Tempest but still she would not submit.

'We…will…try…again.'

And the last turns of her screws brought her level once more.

'Oh, come on, damn you!'

Pulver was not sure if Stebbings plea was addressed to a storm yet to break or to the two ships which had yet to meet in amity. Both would be applicable of course, though the storm when it did break would be a welcome relief as would anything approaching success with the Susannah. A life lived within the Royal Navy was a life built of present successes and not past glories and he was under no illusions that failure in this mission would forever blight a promising career so he did his best to steer Stebbings prayers towards the Susannah and not the storm.

It looked as if his hopes were to be shattered once more as a rain squall, grey and impenetrable, poured liquid darkness over the Bacchante, blinding her even as she made her last approach.

Stebbings once more repeated his curse which this time was rewarded with a furnace hot blast of air and a livid white tongue of flame which leapt from roiling black clouds and plunged with spiked fever into the slate-coloured sea.

The clap of thunder was lost in the noise of the storm which having showed its power refused to relent, blowing yet harder and punishing the sea with more and more savage bolts which caused shadows brief and sharp edged to flicker across the men's faces.

'There could be no hope now', thought Pulver. The Navy had a time-tested method of dealing with failures and he knew that his future life would involve a series of dreary shore appointments and grey-haired retirement.

He was lost in his thoughts for a moment and so missed Stebbings frantic shouts, but at last the Chief Petty Officer, despairing of making himself heard over the storm gripped his officers head and shouted in his ear.

'Fuckin' look, just Look!'

The blasts of hot air and white thunderbolts had cleared the air leaving both ships heaving like untried remounts before battle…but together.

Knot for knot, course for course and with the distance between them not just right but exactly right.

'We did it, we fuckin' did it, look at those bastards!'

Pulver had no need to follow Stebbings pointed arm, he could see oilskinned sailors grip the swaying oil tubes which dangled from the Susannah's outflung stanchions while a series of ropes now linked the ships in temporary sisterhood.

'We did it!'

Stebbings grin vanished for a second as another wave broke over the bow of the Bacchante but it reappeared seconds later broader than ever.

'I knew we could do it; I knew…'

Whatever further words he was about to say died in his throat because Mr. Pulver had set sail for the bridge using the peculiar crab-like walk that sailors use when navigating a heaving deck.

He knew well enough that every member of the bridge would be plundered of their memories of this afternoon's events and each memory would be transformed and tabulated in the curious purple ink which was his officer's own peculiar call sign.

Stebbings knew that it did not really matter what colour ink was used, what mattered and mattered very much was the fact that at long last they had succeeded and succeeded at the height of a storm, and if it could be done in such weather the lessons learnt could be applied in calmer seas.

They'd done it, first they had found how not to do it and applied those bitter lessons to a new day.

There would be other days now, days when a rough-hewn triumph would be polished into gleaming dexterity but he had no fear of such days.

Because they had done it…they had finally done it.

'There you bastard, who is the better ship now? Who won out in the end, who finally put an end to all your tricks? A long obscenity-filled hymn of triumph issued from the Bacchante, fueled and fanned by weeks of frustrating effort but there was no reply from her now linked companion and for a sea mile or more the two ships plunged on through the howling gale until the Bacchante, still basking in her victory and still hurling profanities was shocked when a clear thin voice rang out between them.

'And who, young lady taught you manners? Is that any way to address someone? I have never heard such bad manners in all my life and I never wish to hear them again!'

For a moment the Bacchante looked wildly round to see if a third ship had somehow joined them but there was no one, only the foam headed waves who ran giggling from the rushing wind, the flaring lightning…and the Susannah.

This was a voice far different from the accented sneering voice she was used to hearing and belonged to a patrician woman leaving middle age behind her who had seen much of life and was impressed by very little of what she had seen.

'I can see that your upbringing has not been of the best and that you can hardly be considered at this stage a fit companion for me.'

The statement was made in a level tone by one who not only was used to command, but expected to be obeyed without question which brought forth the obvious question from the Bacchante.

'Who the devil are you?'

'I would have thought that was obvious to the meanest intelligence, young lady. I am the Susannah and I am not impressed either by your profanity or your seamanship. I will make it my duty to curb the former while bringing the latter up to what I consider an acceptable standard. That last attempt was not in any way good enough. Tomorrow we will venture out again and not only will you pay close attention to my instructions, you will do so without profane language. Is that clear?'

The Bacchante carried a full complement of guns and torpedoes and had already won battle honours but was wise enough to recognise a force of nature when she heard one and the Dithmarschen was now firmly the Susannah and most positively fell into that category so there really was only one answer to make.

'Aye, aye Ma'am.'

There was a half disdainful sniff from the Susannah.

'I should certainly hope so. Something may be made of you yet though I suspect you have a hard course to steer. Now I suggest that we immediately seek shelter while I tell you everything that you did wrong today. I ask that you pay close attention because the list of your errors is lamentably long. Firstly....'

It was only at this stage as refined accents listed every error that the Bacchante understand that sometimes defeat was far gentler an option than victory and that her life in future was to be very different.

THE NEXT DECEPTION

The plaudits of a cheering Parliament were all very nice, a spoonful of honey that had flavoured a bland breakfast but the business of the King's government must be carried on and who better to do so than his First Minister?

And where better than the cabinet room of Ten Downing street, a room which had seen every emotion from tears to desk thumping anger. Indeed he had performed both actions in this very room

But today the room was attempting to perform another function; it was attempting to exude power and ultimately to overawe his guests. The polished silverware, the paintings of victorious battles and the men who led them, even the artfully cut sandwiches which lay uneaten, all were designed to show unbroken and unbreakable power. That was its function today, a function that it had only partially accomplished.

He looked round and his eyes met those of Georges Mandel whose eyebrows rose in ironic greeting. There were times when he hated Georges Mandel and today was one of those times, for not only was Mandel unimpressed by his surroundings, he was very politely, but very obviously ignoring the fact that many of the paintings showed victories over his fellow countrymen.

The fact that he was using such gracious diplomacy as a goad to half humorously irritate him was insufficient reason to fuel a rising tide of anger.

No, the reason he was so angry was that Mandel had tempted him, had used his knowledge of how he thought to place before him a plan which cool sanity urged him to reject while the risk-taker which lay not very far beneath his surface reached for with greedy hands. Worse than that, he had attempted to out manoeuvre him.

And that, though it could be forgiven must be punished.

And today was the day a measured amount of punishment would be given.

He looked again at Mandel and the eyebrows rose a little more and an almost imperceptible gallic shrug broke forth.

He broke eye contact and turned to the man who sat at Mandel's side, for here at least he had succeeded.

The man beside him was impressed, and more than a little. Belarmino Tomás was a former miner who headed the Sovereign Council of the Asturian and Basque Republics and Churchill recognised the type of man he was, for he had seen such men before. Vanity, ambition, a way with words and impossible promises had pushed him far higher than those more able and now he was here at the centre of a power that waged war across continents; that very fact fanning the flames of his vanity and inflating his ambition.

Churchill gave an internal shrug; such men were to be treated affably, given every courtesy, but ultimately treated for what they were, a cover, a fig leaf for the two men who sat to the right of Mandel.

Of the two he had decided instantly that he liked Jorge. The man looked like a peasant; broad of shoulder with massive hands that held Downing Street's best china with surprising delicacy and a simple smile that never left a wind-beaten face.

Only when Churchill mentioned Percy Hobart had the smile changed to a wide grin and a laugh that shook the windows. Jorge had reached out and gripped his shoulders with hands that easily encompassed the tailored fabric of Churchill's suit.

'Love him as we do; together we cut the Germans into less than men.'

Churchill shuddered a little at the words, for he knew that for many German soldiers this was literally a fact and the peoples war in Spain had been bloody and without pity. Despite that he had warmed to the man who hid great intelligence behind a simple façade.

His companion though he was not so sure of; indeed truth be told he was glad that he was meeting the man here and not in some other less civilized place. Comandante O'Neil was a conundrum, a jigsaw with several important pieces not quite fitting together.

A cultured man, a man whose first wish on seeing London had been to visit an art gallery and yet despite that there was a bitter ice in the eyes that gazed unblinkingly back at him. Nevertheless the less the man was a valued asset who had built up an extensive intelligence network and exhibited a devilish ingenuity in the black arts of deception and counter intelligence.

It was O'Neil who added the finishing touches to Operation Dogmeat, the Allied plan that convinced the Italians that it was they and not the Greeks who were to be the next to feel the tread of Allied boots.

So far his plan to subdue his guests was not the success he had planned; only one man had succumbed and he held the least value of all. Still he had other means of coercion and he would rely on them.

He coughed and cleared his throat and O'Neil's cold blue eyes gazed back at him.

He was too old a campaigner to let such things distress him, still it would be a great comfort to know what the man was thinking.

A great comfort indeed.

'I shall paint us all, but most of all I shall paint you.'

His brother's words echoed and re-echoed in O'Neil's head as he gazed back at Churchill. He wondered what his brother's eyes would make of the man who sat before him. Would they paint the hanging jowls, the loose skin that announced advancing years, or would he paint the idea of the man, the spirit that even now glowed forth?

He would never know, for those eyes had long since been closed by death, and though much blood had been spilt between that day and this still his guilt gnawed at him.

Yet his brother lived on.

On war's approach the British had acted. While guns roared and searchlights probed the dark in practice for the trial to come men had come to the galleries and the exhibits and taken the great art works far, far away to live out the war safe from bomb and fire.

And yet the Rembrandts, the Turners and the Da Vincis all must be replaced for art must ever be placed before the people and other lesser artists took the place of the great masters.

Hugh O'Neil never knew how a single example of his brother's art came to be hanging where once the agony of Christ had hung, but one day while outside the rain poured he stood bareheaded while staring at a portrait of his grandfather.

To see his brother's art hanging from such a renowned wall was a bittersweet moment, for in truth this was a whispered ambition only now fulfilled, and yet there would be no others for the hands that impelled these brushstrokes were stilled forever and every other work had been culled by the scythe of war.

For a moment his demons lay still, quieted by hot tears and a power that used line and brushstroke to reach across the years and break Time's bond.

But only for a moment, and he turned and walked out into the rain hoping without hope that it would cleanse from him a little of his anguish.

It was not to be and he threw himself into his work, for to deceive the enemy was every much as hurtful as spilling his blood and he worked now with a red-headed man who called himself a Major but obviously held high rank within the councils of war.

Here the web of intrigue he had built up was supercharged by a far greater power with far greater resources and together they began to sow doubt in the minds of Rome.

His brother would be proud of him, for his brushstrokes were very fine and very delicate.

A word in the wrong ear, whole armies fabricated from thin air, a thousand flights that flew and clicked the seeking camera.

All these things and more he used to convince that hammer blows were coming from a white-hot forge.

And a last coup where a growing Asturian navy employed a dead man, a moonless night and a favourable tide.

Close in to a captured French coast they sailed, scattering artfully cut parts of aircraft and a man who had one last service to perform. Clothed in the right uniform, equipped with papers that verified, he was dropped with a last prayer into the water where a running tide took him to a patrolled beach.

There his chained briefcase confirmed every fear, proved every guess and Italy trembled anew while her northern cities were occupied by grey-clad legions, the better to protect them from phantom armies.

O'Neil's demons shouted with joy for the enemy did their bidding and danced to their tune.

But that was then and this was now.

He sat between Mandel and Jorge, friend to one but merely ally to the other. Mandel would never be a friend, just a man to use even as he used O'Neil, but never, ever to be trusted, always to be given a second glance.

Georges Mandel served only two things and two things only.

The first was George Mandel, for beneath that patient exterior burned an ambition that could never be extinguished. And in fairness that ambition was harnessed to serve the second thing that Mandel worshipped.

France…or at least the version of France that Mandel wished to rise from the ruins of the old.

To nurture that new France he had plotted and schemed for in the world to come he had seen much danger and many enemies.

And if there was much danger and a host of foes for France how much more so for the nations which had formed out of the wreckage of Spain? Such had been his argument that day as they watched Franco pace in his cage.

The seeds of a secret alliance had been sown that day, naturally he had told Jorge and just as naturally he had not told Belarmino Tomás, for the man was in his eyes no more than a useful tool whose loyalty was a best variable.

Many of Tomás's companions were even now languishing on a windswept Scottish island, possibly regretting their allegiance to Moscow and lamenting the day that they had ever heard of Joseph Stalin.

The fact that this had caused a minor rift between the western and eastern halves of the alliance was of no concern to him; he had promised the exiles death if they ever returned to Spain and he had every intention of fulfilling that promise, personally if at all possible.

He did not know if this new scheme of Mandel's would work; certainly it wasn't part of the discussions they had long ago; it seemed a chance thing, a random event that he was attempting to weave into a complicated tapestry.

Still he saw no reason why the plan should not go ahead despite its slim chances of success. There was very little risk, at least to Asturias and it was up to Mandel to persuade.

There was a rattle of china and he looked over to where Jorge placed a now empty cup on the highly polished table.

For a moment their eyes met and he knew exactly what Jorge was thinking.

If he could get out of this damned room, Jorge thought, I would be a damned sight happier. London appalled him, it was crowded, dirty, busy and smelled. Its people never made eye contact and seemed never to say exactly what they were thinking. He longed for fresh air and views that consisted of white-capped mountains and not grey-faced buildings. The sooner he stood on a mountainside with a keen wind blowing through him the better he would feel.

Yet there was much to do before that day and this being so he sat wearing an unwanted uniform adorned with unwanted medals

These meetings were part victory celebrations and part strategy meetings; the Fascists were bleeding from a score of wounds and soon would receive the massive blow which would send them into Death's arms.

Asturias had been asked to take part. Yet how could she?

Years of war had reduced her to gauntness; aged grandmothers and young children worked side by side in the rubble with the few that could be spared.

There were men and women, that was true, and all were veterans - that was true also - but they watched the borders and guarded against unrest to the south and enmity to the north.

Asturias and their brother Basques were pygmies, exhausted blood bathed pygmies that had played their part and now must bathe their wounds and watch the giants contend.

To ask for more was impossible and unfair.

Hugh had told him Mandel's plans and he had agreed. Asturias needed a future and it needed allies, even ones he did not quite trust. But he certainly did not like this latest plan; though in truth the reason he did not like it is that it sprang from a fouled spring.

The Vatican had expressed several thoughts and Mandel, he of the agile and serpentine mind, had picked up those ideas and added his own particular lustre.

And it was the source that bothered him for he hated the Church.

It had not only stood by when his people had been butchered and starved, but had told the foulest lies about the war, absolving in the name of God every atrocity and every episode of butchery.

Like many in his land he had turned away from the Church and had only curses for it. It had taken much persuasion before he would agree to release even a grudging acceptance of Mandel's ideas.

He comforted himself with the thought that soon this journey would be over and he would be able to stride through the long grass of home. Soon he would be away from smoke and noise and thrice-damned politicians.

He glanced over at Mandel as this last thought ran through his mind and received a brief smile in return.

Mandel's smile to Jorge was genuine enough for he had much admiration for the man, but despite that he knew that Jorge had many misgivings over the ideas he had proposed.

Of course, when he received the message from Cardinal Montini, Mandel had dismissed it as an impossible request and had already formed in his head the phrases which would form a polite denial.

And yet.

Two cigarettes later the first of the ideas had come to the surface, slowly like reluctant bubbles in a sparkling wine, but the idea was sound enough and there were details still to be added and even more importantly permissions given for though he had risen far still he was not quite master of his destiny yet.

And that was the first problem, he had agreed that Italy was to be deceived, she was to be starved and she was to be bombed and shelled but there was to be no mainland invasion, no landings or expeditions.

He had agreed, on behalf of Free France he had agreed that Fascist Italy would be left to collapse, forcing their German allies to spend ever thinning resources propping up a regime that was far too weak to stand on its own.

He had agreed.

And yet, and yet.

What if there was a way to give Italy a thin chance to grasp a shred of stability?

The France to come…his France, would need secure borders.

There was nothing he could do about her southern borders. The best he could do was to co-opt the Asturians and Basques into a rough alliance which could be built on later. But an Italy left to her own devices might well descend into anarchy and anarchy had a distressing habit of spreading and even if it did not an unstable Italy would be a perennial source of friction to France.

Montini's letter raised many problems - political, military and a disturbing personal one which brought forth shivers of distaste. For a moment he was back in a collapsing France, hearing the news that the army of Belgium had been ordered to lay down their arms. He remembered the disbelieving fear, the shouts and the curses directed at one man. And now he was asked to aid that man to rescue him from a comfortable, but deserved captivity.

And yet, if he could swallow distaste much could be gained…for France.

The military problems he had given over to Hugh O'Neil, while he had turned his thoughts to the political ones. He had come up with answers, though not solutions which is why they were here today

And yet there was a chance, the risk was a small one and he lost little by asking…perhaps.

Churchill coughed, cleared his throat and the conversation began.

'The first question I must ask Georges is whatever possessed you to come up with such an idea and why you have come to me. There are after all channels for this sort of thing.'

Mandel ignored the aggrieved tone in Churchill's voice. It could be real or it could be mere mockery for the man was a consummate actor, but real or not he was committed to a set course and had no choice but to carry on.

'The channels seem to be blocked Winston. Besides which the matter is urgent.'

'So you say, Georges, so you say. Yet I too received a similar message from the cardinal. So I gather did the Americans, yet neither of us gave the matter more than a few seconds of consideration. But you did…Why is that I wonder?'

'I saw a chance to help the Italian people, Winston, no more than that.'

'Really Georges? You expect me to believe that in a burst of altruism, you conceived and polished…if I may use the word loosely this absurd plan solely to help the poor, put-upon Italians? Would it not be fairer to say that you saw an opportunity to meddle in Italian politics…to your benefit I might add, and you clothed that opportunity in the ill-fitting clothes of philanthropy?'

'That is a little unkind Winston.'

Churchill was unimpressed by Mandel's protests of innocence and waved a dismissive cigar. 'But the facts will bear that interpretation, Georges, and to make matters worse you attempt to co-opt others into your schemes.' He turned his eyes towards Jorge who was looking increasingly uncomfortable. 'Tell me Jorge, what are your thoughts on the matter?'

Jorge's answer was a conflicted rumble. 'I do not know this Montini. He has sent no letter to me, but I know the servants of his church and know them well. They told people to bless the bombs that fell on them, blamed and cursed them for fighting the invaders and told lies that their own eyes would deny. We of Asturias are no friends of this church, nor of the Italians who entered our lands without invite and now lie in cold graves.

'We were asked to provide plans that would allow all that this cardinal has asked; this we have done. As to the wisdom of carrying out these plans I cannot say, for I am a simple peasant.'

Jorge paused, never taking his eyes from Churchill's. 'Two things more I will say. First, I would say that I do not trust this man; he speaks of a great suffering to come, yet it is not his suffering alone that concerns him, but the survival of his position and all he holds dear. His words are fair, but to my mind he speaks for a wolf and every wolf has teeth.

'However even as a wolf he has raised a fair point, your plans for Italy leave her abandoned and wounded, prey to those who would rend her, prey to both friend and foe. This sounds like civil war, something I know a great deal about.

'Mr. Churchill in war it is the soldier who risks his life, but in a civil war all are at risk. The old,the sick, the young, the old…all are at risk. I have shot Italians, I have killed Italians, but with Italian grandmothers I have no quarrel. I do not know if Montini can persuade this princess from Belgium to act, I do not know if her voice will be heeded. But if you

34

act, act for your interests and not his, if you do something, do it for the grandmother and not the cleric.'

He paused, a little embarrassed at having said so much and shrugged his shoulders. 'I'm sorry not to be of more help but then I am a peasant and do not understand such things.'

Churchill had listened very carefully to words which mirrored his own thoughts and laughed at Jorge's last words. The man was anything but simple, for all his peasant birth.

It was time to begin Mandel's punishment and he turned once more to the pale-faced Frenchman.

'So, Georges what do you think of that, has not our Asturian friend come straight to the heart of the matter? The Vatican after many long years of, if not outright condoning Fascism, then certainly ignoring its barbarity, has now seen which way the wind is blowing and wishes to trim its sails accordingly. It rightly guesses that the replacement of Signor Mussolini with a cabal of slightly less unsavoury characters would be rejected by the Allies and looks around for someone to save its neck and so it reaches out.

'Only you, for reasons of your own respond, but you are not strong enough yet to act on your own, so you ask our Asturian friends here to come up with plans to suit your purpose, thinking that in this way you may avoid altogether the planning departments set up specifically for such events. The Asturians, puzzled no doubt but anxious to please, bend to your will and come up with the folders that now lie before us.'

Churchill's cigar glowed an angry red.

'It won't do Georges. It won't do at all. You have over reached yourself and over reached badly.'

He opened the first of many folders and pretended to study its contents.

'Montini suggests that that in order to make Princess Marie more amenable to our cause we rescue her brother, the King of the Belgians from German captivity.'

The folder was closed with finality and he put a heavy note of sarcasm in his voice. 'Leaving aside the fact that this is the very same king who betrayed us in nineteen forty, leaving aside the fact that this same king refused to go into exile and is now seriously at odds with his own government and leaving aside the fact that the king has made no effort

35

to escape from his most comfortable imprisonment, there is the fact that even Commandante O'Neil who you tasked with planning the rescue described the operation as having very little chance of success. I would go further, for if I am honest, I feel very little need today for diplomacy.'

A heavy hand slammed down on the folder.

'This would be a suicide mission which would go very wrong, very quickly. An assault on a heavily guarded royal palace on the outskirts of a major city is plainly ridiculous. Even if our forces managed to defeat the German guards, even if they persuade the King to leave with them, they still have to fight their way through a now thoroughly aroused garrison. There is also the very real possibility that the king may be killed during the operation, which I should not have to remind you would be a political disaster for the allies generally and me personally.'

The folder was picked up and placed with no great delicacy in a wire tray.

'This operation dies right now. I will hear no more of it…do you understand me Georges? No more military adventures planned in secret, Georges…No matter how heartfelt the cause.'

Churchill looked at his guests; Tomás was obviously impressed by this show of force from one leader to another, while Jorge had clearly enjoyed the argument. Hugh O'Neil had not allowed a flicker of emotion to show, while Georges Mandel sat with thin lips as his hopes were torn to shreds.

He had shown his tiger's eyes but now it was time to bring Mandel back into the fold. 'Georges, I once had the honour to meet the King's father before his most unfortunate death; he was a man of high courage and great honour who shared his people's misfortunes with humour, fortitude and compassion. His son has not followed that path. I cannot say how that affords with his personal honour, nor with the high office with which he has been blessed. What I can say is that I will not risk good men to save a worse, no matter how grateful his sister may be. Besides which it is not up to us to prove our good intentions, for we have proved them times without number. It is up to her to prove her intentions. It is up to her and it is up to Cardinal Montini to act as he sees fit.

'However nether of them can act at the moment as the Cardinal resides in Rome while the Princess has fled for safety, taking her children with her. She now resides in the mountains near the village of Sarre close to the borders of Switzerland and France. There she is safe, but it can only be a fleeting safety for she cannot escape the attention of the Germans who have occupied most of Northern Italy believing we intend to invade.'

For a moment there was a fleeting expression of satisfaction on O'Neil's face and then it vanished while Churchill continued.

'I note that there is a subsidiary plan which involves spiriting her and her family from that place and taking them to a more secure location. That plan will go ahead. However, Georges, it will be an Allied plan in which you may take your share and only your share of credit.'

A last glow from the cigar saw it extinguished which matched the smothering of Mandel's dreams.

'Again, Georges. I hope I am understood?'

Mandel could only nod as Churchill gifted him a beaming smile of forgiveness but not forgetfulness.

'Excellent, now Jorge, I believe you had some thoughts on this plan?'

Jorge's voice rumbled round the room while he explained just who he would send and why.

Churchill listened attentively, contenting himself with only the occasional grunt of agreement, Jorge's plan was relatively simple and needed only a very small contribution from others. It would be Asturias's first expedition outside the borders of Spain and Churchill made thankful noises.

It was at this point that Belarmino Tomás spoke. With grand words and eloquent gestures he described how pleased he was that the Asturian and Basque Republics were able to help, and that as junior members of the grand coalition they were willing to make every sacrifice.

Churchill ignored the appalled look Jorge cast and the icy daggers that O'Neil threw. This was his chance; he had not misjudged Tomás, and this was his chance.

'I am glad you say such things Signor Tomás, for I am sure that we would welcome the battle-hardened regiments of the brother republics.

I understood that there were some difficulties and objections, but I now see that they have all been swept away.'

Having pounced he turned back to Jorge. He had been victorious over Tomás and Mandel today but there was no need to antagonise a man for whom he had deep respect. 'When the time comes, as come it must, you will serve alongside your old friend General Hobart. I hope you will agree to that?'

Jorge had been outmanoeuvred and could only give rueful agreement, though after this meeting was over there would be a small discussion with Tomás where his main concern would be stopping O'Neil tearing Tomás limb from limb.

However, that would be later, for now he must issue orders.

And that was how Yves Massu, formerly a Sergent-Chef in the Chasseurs Alpins, now senior Sergeant in the Second Guards Regiment of the Asturian Republic came to receive new instructions.

THE MOUNTAIN MAN

Yves Massu had always loved the mountains, loved their snow- capped tops and the cold draughts that flew pure and straight onto the valleys below.

Always he had loved the mountains though the living they gave was a thin one and there was little room for a second son who could find no work in the hungry years that ravaged France.

The army took him and with rare wisdom sent him to where his love of the mountains would serve the Third Republic. In the Chasseurs Alpins he flourished and rose to the rank of Sergent-Chef and there he would have stayed but for war's interruption.

Too late was he called to aid faltering battalions and France fell before his rifle saw even a single enemy.

A stubborn mountain courage flared within him and with comrades at his side he marched south over the peaks that nature had given France to mark her border.

There he was received with joy for a like spirit burned with roaring flame.

The Second Guards Regiment of the Asturian Republic became his new home and there he met new comrades, brothers from conquered Poland, siblings from vanished Czechoslovakia. A thousand men from lands far and near, men who sought to kill, sought revenge.

They were scouts and saboteurs, killers in the dark, creatures of fable and shadow. To spy out the land ahead, to slip unseen, to steal an enemy's comfort and his life were acts well-polished that forced fear into enemy throats. But victory brought only borders that must be held and not crossed lest his birthland be prodded from her sleep and forced to turn active enmity into actual war.

The Second Guards Regiment became much depleted now war's press pushed less hard and many left to join the Free French forces of Georges Mandel but Massu remained, for the sands of North Africa held little attraction for a man who lived for the mountains. Besides which, there was a widow, although in truth this was no rare thing for Northern Spain was a place full of the bereaved. Widows and widowers, orphans and the aged; the land was littered with the broken and the alone.

But the same strength that had seen a people destroy an invader now flowed along a different stream and war's grim machine wove new families out of old.

The widow met the widower, the single man met the woman who wore the bright red badge of one who had lost a mate to the enemy. A thousand and more combinations and no matter what the link all adopted the orphan or aided those who could with honour claim a new nations aid.

Yves and his widow had adopted two children and a grandmother whose family had been butchered. There were no papers to signify this bonding; there was no time and no need, only the urge to heal and to show the world an undaunted spirit.

And life went on. There was little time for the climbing of mountains for there were borders to patrol and a nation's broken bones to help knit and in truth a life where there was a small measure of domestic comfort was a welcome relief.

But he was still a soldier and when ordered to report he brushed a much-used uniform, kissed the widow goodbye, bade his newly-made family farewell and made his way through streets that were slowly being cleared of rubble by people who used bare hands in place of machines.

The headquarters of the Second Guards Regiment was once a peaceful building set well back from the road and only that fact had saved it from the stick of bombs that had demolished its neighbours.

In time it would be returned to its owners, but for now it had adopted a military costume and draped itself with sentries and camouflage.

A short walk down a corridor brought him to the colonel's secretary who ushered him into the inner office with a brief smile for the regiment was as much a family as a military unit and a common cause had welded each man and each woman to the other in bonds that would last far longer than life itself.

Massu stood to attention in the office and the colonel motioned to a worn chair while he read from a folder which had a bright red band emblazoned across it.

Yves looked around the room. A poster of a clenched fist crushing a Nazi cross adorned one wall while a German sergeant's tunic complete with bullet holes hung from another. His colonel's hatred of anything German was well known and the tunic testified to a man who led not from a desk but from the front line. But it was the photograph which interested him the most.

It was not posed but had taken the subjects unaware; a dark-haired woman whose lustrous eyes shone with love was holding the hand of a girl perhaps four years old who had the half smile of a child caught in innocent mischief. The girl held a sadly mutilated doll which in the pursuit of some childhood whim had been shorn of the hair on one side of its head.

It was a pretty picture and one well-known to him, for every member of the regiment had a copy and each was instructed to ask every stranger they met if they had seen the woman or the girl.

Massu shook his head silently, the tales of miraculous reunions had long since dwindled and died…there were too many hasty graves across too wild a country. The colonel's wife and child were undoubtably dead and he could only hope that their end had been quick and without pain.

A cough ended his thoughts. The colonel had put down the folder and was gazing at him. Yves stiffened in his seat while the colonel tapped the folder with long fingers.

'Sergeant Massu, we, that is the regiment have been asked to perform a most unusual mission.'

Massu's first thought was that at last the border was to be breached and his homeland would once more feel the tramp of his boots and his heart rose as the colonel continued. 'We have been asked to escort a lady and her family out of Italy and bring her here.'

The colonel looked deeply troubled and once looked down at the folder once more tapping it with agitated fingers.

'Exactly why has not been revealed to me, but the fact remains that I have been told to do so. The mission is either one for the entire regiment or one man. For obvious reasons I am not about to lead my men in a suicide mission, so I have chosen one man and that man, Sergeant Massu is you.'

For a moment there was silence between the two men as the colonel waited to see if there was a reply and Massu wondered how he was expected to perform the duties of an entire regiment.

The colonel, seeing that there was to be no reply opened up the folder and revealed the photograph of a startlingly beautiful woman.

'This is Princess Marie José who has exiled herself to a royal castle on the Italian border with France. Your mission, Sergeant is to retrieve this woman and bring her safely back here. From there she will be handed over to the British who will take charge of her.'

A slightly embarrassed sigh escaped from the colonel's mouth.

'There are complications, Sergeant which is why I have picked you. You have a habit of not letting complications get in your way.

'Firstly, the woman is married to the heir to the Italian throne. I am told that there is a rift between her and her Father-in-Law and this is the reason for her exile. Secondly, she has small children and they too are to be brought here. Thirdly and most importantly, the whole of Northern Italy is crawling with Nazis and there is near rebellion in the major cities. It can only be a matter of time before she is captured and returned.

'You therefore will gather her up, collect her children and guide her back before she is taken by the Germans or Italian Fascists.'

The folder was opened and Massu was shown a map with a scrawling red line traced over it. 'You will be met at every step of your journey and guided, for it is safer that way.'

Massu nodded his understanding; George Mandel's agents had long since combined forces with those of Commandante O'Neil to fight against German counter intelligence and both kept more than a wary eye open against those Frenchmen whose true allegiance lay in Berlin or Moscow.

He would journey along a path where treachery and betrayal was a well-worn currency and common sense dictated that the less contact he had with those warring tribes the safer he would be, athough in truth if captured he had only to tell the tale unfolding before him to be dismissed as a madman and therefore harmless. He looked into his colonel's eyes and saw the same disquiet reflected there, but both were soldiers and if a colonel had to obey orders how much less choice did a mere sergeant have?

The map was put to one side revealing a handsome castle set within manicured gardens guarded on three sides by the flanks of a mountain range. Massu thought that he had never seen such a handsome building - just the place for an exiled princess to seek shelter; small enough to not attract too much attention, large enough to provide comfort.

'This', said the colonel, pointing at the photograph, '…is the castle of Sarre. There is a village nearby and the castle no doubt has a large staff but you need not concern yourself with them. In the village is your next guide.'

A further photograph showed a smooth-shaven cleric and a grimace of distaste crossed the colonels face.

'Your contact there is a Catholic priest who is confessor and confidante to the Princess.'

Massu heard the animosity in the man's voice. Like many Asturians the colonel had rejected the religion that had sided with Franco, and many Asturian priests had fled to the Basque Republic or those parts of Navarre held by the new republics where they were tolerated but never fully trusted.

Massu shrugged, he considered himself a good man as far as the war would allow, but had long since dispensed with the faith of his childhood, particularly its injunctions against killing.

His creed was a simple one and one followed by soldiers of every age.

Survive.

If the priest was a true man he would live; if he attempted any falsehood he would die for there were very few shades of grey in Sergeant Massu's creed.

The colonel looked across to Massu, wondering if his words had affected the sergeant, but again there was no response from the man so he put to one side his distaste at the involvement of a hated enemy and carried on giving instructions.

'Once you have made contact with the priest, you will be introduced to the princess. You will make whatever arrangements you think necessary for her comfort and you will retrace your steps, returning her and her family to this headquarters.'

The disquiet in the colonel's eyes grew and he fidgeted uncomfortably in his chair. 'Sergeant, I do not know why this woman is considered so important. Nor do I see why family arguments amongst Italian aristocrats should concern us here in Spain, but I have my orders and now you have yours. However, I will give you a further order, one I give not as a colonel but as a friend and one who has seen too many good men die for our cause. This is my order, Yves.

'Come back.

'If you have to abandon the woman then do so' If you have to leave her children in a snow drift, then do not think twice;

'Come back.

'There are too few of us now to care about strangers and you have a new family to think of and all the duties that go with that family.'

There was a broken sigh from the colonel and he looked at the photograph that a stubborn and hopeful spirit refused to wrap in black ribbon. 'Families are important, so I order you to think of yours before all else. You will leave tonight. There will be time for last farewells.'

A wave of regret and anxiety ran through Massu for he was leaving a new-forged family behind but then his widow was a veteran of the Navarrese border war and the three Italian crosses burnt into the stock of her rifle were grim testament to her talents at survival.

'The regiment looks after its own.'

The colonel had watched his sergeant's face and guessed at the thoughts which were running through Massu's head; his words did not need to be said, for they were undoubtably true, but the act of saying them was a promise, not Colonel to Sergent but one man to another. It was a comforting thought that swirled through his head as it made his way to the small room that held the widow, the grandmother and two girls. His family would be safe, come what may they would be safe.

But there were other thoughts, some tinged with joy, some with doubt.

He had always loved the mountains and journey's end would see him tread high peaks once more and feel crisp air in a savouring mouth.

And all his elation at these thoughts there were other darker ones that sprang up like horrid toadstools. It seemed he had been transported to a fairy tale, with Nazis for dragons and Italian Fascists playing the part of evil witches while he was to perform the duties of a knight errant

44

and rescue the Princess from the castle. The problem was that, as the son of a peasant, he was under-equipped to perform such duties. Besides, he more than half suspected that such duties involved kissing princesses and this he was sure would not meet with the approval of his widow.

He did his best to banish such thoughts. The future was unknown and more than capable of looking after itself.

But he was going back to the mountains.

And that was joy enough to banish a thousand dragons.

TRANSPORTATION BY SEA

'Two red, one white, three red. That's them all right.'

The voice belonged to an ugly man with a broken nose, untameable stubble and a forehead marked with a thin white scar where a bullet from a dying Nationalist cruiser had drawn blood. That was in the dark days when the Asturian Navy was little more than these two torpedo boats plus twin fountains of hope and courage.

Now he commanded a bigger fleet that sallied forth to bar the U-boats safe passage across Biscay waves and his days were spent not on a rocking deck, but on dry land where he studied battle reports and fought not an enemy made of flesh and steel but one made of paper and words. Truly he was far too young for such a burden but in an Asturias thinned by war he led by default and gave the same devotion to desk and chair that he once gave to deck and gun.

But a young spirit cannot long be held and tonight he had chosen to mount an old steed, for there was none to gainsay him. A brief holiday at sea would clean the smell of office dust from his soul and so the torpedo boats, La Constitución and La Independencia were slipped from their berths and sped through a star-dusted night to the very edge of the shores of conquered France carrying their leader, their crews and a single passenger.

Yes, a small holiday, with perhaps a little hunting on the return journey, for who knows what chance may throw his way? But first he must deliver his passenger.

For Yves Massu the last few hours had been filled with emotions.

There was the heart rush that came from the knowledge that once more he would return to the land of his birth, the controlled dread that every soldier must feel at the unsheathing of swords and the pangs of leaving a family formed from the residues of war. A mingling of emotions had been his lot but now at this very moment he felt but one emotion and that was misery.

The cause was not hard to decipher. Massu was a land creature and the sea and this accursed toy boat had combined to cause his stomach to heave and roll in time with the pitch of the waves.

He lent over the rail and the sea received the last few dregs of an insulted stomach while his shoulder felt the impact of a salt-hardened hand.

'Do not worry my friend, there is a cure for your suffering and it is close at hand. Look! See how they signal. Soon you will be on dry land and all will be well.'

Massu lifted up bleary, sorrow-raddled eyes and saw the lights flicker red and white from the shore and tried to show some interest. The sailor had promised him relief from his sickness and that was indeed good though any relief including death would be welcomed with open arms just now.

'Seek the shade of an oak tree, Sergeant, for that is the best cure I know.'

The shoulder flexed and lifted a limp Massu to his feet, deposited him in a small boat and bade him farewell.

If the torpedo boat had been torture then the dinghy was a compressed hell, for it took a malicious pleasure in pointing its bows first up to the dark sky and then down to a dark sea bed but there were no amateurs in the Asturian navy and a trembling, wet and bedraggled Massu was safely deposited on a shingle beach that hissed its anger at an encroaching tide.

For the second time that night friendly hands gripped him and a dimmed light shone in his face.

'You must come with me.'

There were no more words, but the hands impelled him up the beach and into a small house that perched precariously at the very edge of the rocks.

Massu looked around. This was obviously a fisherman's cottage; rope and cordage was coiled neatly in a corner, while nets and oilskins hung from the rafters. A driftwood fire smoked and sparked in the centre of the room and Massu was pushed, none too gently, towards its warmth by the man who had greeted him at the beach.

An old man.'

Massu guessed the man would be nearer eighty than seventy and a life lived close to the sea had riven great lines in his face and left only a few strands of hair on his head.

The old man looked at him with a curious half-smile on his head which he cocked to one side, looking for all the world like an inquisitive bird that had spied something particularly interesting.

'My name is Unax and you must obey me for I am the mayor!'

Massu was about to make a reply when the old man sprang towards a cabinet and drew forth a great brass bound helmet which he drew over his head until it hid his eyes.

'My name is Unax and you must obey me for I am the fire chief!'

The helmet was dashed to the ground and the man burrowed into a pile of clothing pulling out a gendarme's waterproof cape and stiff brimmed hat.

'I am Unax the policeman, come to arrest the Boche!'

The uniform followed the helmet to the floor and the old man claimed to be priest, butcher, baker and carpenter without pausing to take breath.

Massu had entirely forgotten his sickness and was wondering what he should do if the old man attacked him and if his mission had ended in failure before it had even begun when the old man subsided into his seat at the dinner table, placed his head in his hands and began to weep.

At last a tear stained face looked up.

'They are all gone. The Mayor, the priest, our gendarme, the village council, all gone. I buried them at night because I was afraid they would come back and they did come back but I was clever and hid and they didn't find me, oh no I was too clever for them! But I kept the clothes and that way I will live. I, Unax will be the mayor and the policeman and the priest and that means that when they come back they cannot kill me for I am already dead.'

The man was mad Massu decided. Whether he had been mad for a long time or this was a recent occurrence was impossible to say, but a series of questions brought mumbling answers which formed a picture.

The cottage was a little distance from the village and the village was of course Basque for the Basques had long ago settled this part of France.

The Germans, unable to defeat the Spanish Basques had vented their spite on the French Basques and the old man had been a witness to a small part of that retribution.

The leading citizens of the village had been shot, the rest rounded up and taken who knows where, leaving only a bewildered and accidental survivor. But the old man mentioned that there were good men who came and brought food and it was those men who had trained him in the use of the coloured lights.

There was little else of sense to be got out of the old man and Massu threw more driftwood on the fire and a threadbare blanket over the now sleeping old man.

His stomach which had spent the past few hours rejecting every morsel of food, had with great perversity began to demand that he feed it, but a search of the room revealed not a morsel of food.

Massu was a tired, hungry and a little angry that his journey had begun so poorly, but as a soldier he had learnt patience and that teaching he put into practice. He wrapped a dead gendarme's cape around himself and joined the old man in sleep.

It was the soft scuffle of stones that woke him hours later as the last of the night fled before the first of the day. He was a light sleeper, lighter than the mad old man who still snored softly before a dying fire, waking up only when an insistent hand demanded that the door be opened.

The old man leapt to his feet and an open door revealed two figures who found themselves looking at the open mouth of Massu's pistol.

The younger of the two men gave a disdainful glance at Massu and gave a little fatalistic shrug. 'Either shoot us or put the gun down.'

He did not bother waiting for an answer but strode into the room and shook the old man's hand.

'Mr. Mayor?

A vigorous nodding of the head showed that he had guessed this morning's alter ego.

'You did well, Mr. Mayor, very well indeed; we have brought food.'

The second man thrust a bound cloth into the hands of Unax who tore it open to reveal a half loaf of hard bread and a few lumps of harder cheese which was soon crammed into a hungry mouth.

Massu's stomach rumbled in envy and the young man grinned the grin of one who had eaten recently. A silent signal resulted in Massu receiving the rest of the bread and cheese plus a half bottle of rough wine which he consumed with as much decorum as an empty stomach would allow while the young man watched him with a sort of wary playfulness.

Unax had finished his meal and was pacing back and forth between piles of clothing muttering to himself with increasing agitation. For a moment the young man gazed at him with amusement glittering in his eyes until tiring of the sight he reached out and halted the old man in mid stride.

'Perhaps Monsieur le gendarme should take a turn around the village. We look to him to keep us safe in our beds.'

Unax bobbed his head in excited agreement, grabbing the hat and cape, mimicking the appearance of a diligent officer of the law. A smile of appreciation to Unax was coupled with a nod to the second man and both left leaving the young man to shrug his shoulder in resignation.'

'What would you have me do? I am neither a doctor or a nursemaid, we feed him as best we can and we have trained him to do simple tasks, for if there is danger or a trap it is better that he dies or is captured than me or my men. His life is of no great value even to himself and I pity the man who would try to interrogate him.

'So, it was last night. We watched from a distance and stood guard while you slept, but now it is morning, you have slept and it is time to turn to business. I do not know your name and you have no need of mine. All you need to know is that I am in charge of your first steps of your journey.'

There was the sound of a truck outside and Massu was guided outside to where an ancient vehicle blew black smoke into the morning air. The young man got in beside his companion leaving Massu to sit beside the window. A wire crate containing two scrawny chickens was thrust into his lap and he threw a questioning glance at the young man only to receive a bitter laugh in return.

'It is the chicken tax my friend. When the Germans took my people away, they took away our ability to feed our conquerors. There are too few of us now; a handful of farmers, a few bakers and butchers; barely enough for us to live.'

They were passing through an eerily quiet village now and Massu could see doors left open, grass growing in the streets and the tattered remains of clothes still pegged to rotting lines.

The young man noticed Massu's eyes staring at the sight.

'All that is left are those like me who do what they can and old mad men who must play many parts.'

They were driving past Unax now, still dressed in the uniform of a murdered policeman. He threw them a smart salute and received an airy wave from the driver.

'So, you must pay the chicken tax. Not all our captors are Aryan supermen, for Hitler fights on many fronts and the young and the fit fight where the fighting is hardest. Here in the Basque country we have a few supermen, but we have many who are fit only for occupation duties; the halt and the lame, the old and the unfit.

'It is their weakness and our strength. Many of these men wish only to survive and return to their families. Their rations do not make them fat and a chicken or perhaps some vegetables results in only a brief inspection.'

They were passing through a land of small fields now and though Massu was no farmer he could see that they were ill-tended; choked with weeds, with ditches overfull and hedgerows straggling with uncut branches.

The young man noticed his gaze.

'They are a blight these Germans; worse than locusts; for locusts kill to eat and the Germans kill from lust, but we will rise again. When the war ends the Basques will return and rule themselves within a free France and a great road will be built between ourselves and our Spanish brothers. This has been promised to us, though in truth we would fight in any case, for what choice do we have?

'I wished to cross the mountains and fight as many of us did, but my mother was against the idea and I could not leave her alone. Now my mother is gone and I have my fight without the inconvenience of crossing mountains.'

The words were spoken conversationally and Massu could detect no anger or bitterness in them. There was no need to ask where the young man's mother had gone, ruined fields and empty villages gave testament enough to her fate, but the calmness in her son's voice made Massu wonder if this too was another form of madness, another way of dealing with an impossible situation.

There was no time to ponder further on these thoughts for there was a warning hiss from the driver and Massu saw a red-striped pole blocking the road and three German soldiers.

The truck obediently slowed and stopped with Massu pulling his cap low down on his head. Papers were handed over and the glass on Massu's side was tapped by a soldier with a rifle slung over his shoulder.

'Hand over the chickens', again the voice was calm, betraying no sense of fear or anxiety, 'and smile while you do it.'

Massu wound down his window and handed over the chickens to a sergeant who sported a livid scar that ran from his neck along a shattered jaw and up through a sightless left eye.

The hand that gripped the wire basket was missing two fingers and trembled more than the cold mountain-born wind would deserve. There was grunt from the sergeant and then orders that came from a mouth equipped with ill-fitting dentures; the pole was raised and with a grinding of gears the truck continued along the road towards the town.

'You have cost me two good chickens. I hope you are worth it', was the only comment from the young man and the men lapsed into silence while the truck continued to belch black smoke down an almost empty road.

At last they began the approach into a small town and Massu began to see some signs of life. There were open shops and a gendarme who directed traffic with an imperious whistle. A white-gloved hand gave them release and the truck pulled up at a small railway station which had obviously been designed and built on a fixed-cost basis.

Ignoring the architectural deficiencies, the driver got out and the young man signalled that for Massu this was his intended destination. Without explanation he was handed a battered suitcase and a train ticket.

The calm voice floated through the open window of the truck. 'Remember, you owe me two good chickens!'

And with that the truck left, leaving him in a cloud of black smoke and wondering if every French Basque was as mad as the sample he had seen so far.

Still he had been delivered to the town of Dax, the second leg of his journey was over and the third part was about to begin. He had a train ticket, a suitcase and a false identity. And what more could a sergeant in the Second Guards Regiment want?

'Cousin Émile, it is so good to see you!'

It was late evening and Massu was now at a slightly larger railway station and almost before he had taken in the scene he was wrapped in huge arms that pushed the air out of his lungs leaving him powerless to resist while a voice like a great bell rang in his ear. 'Say as little as possible, we are being watched.'

The arms released him and Massu staggered back a little without their support and on recovering looked up at a giant of a man who stood a little under two metres tall and with immense shoulders.

A face framed by a great spade-shaped beard and bushy eyebrows held two bright blue eyes which looked down on him with concern. He had obviously dressed for the occasion, wearing a collar and tie that had tried but failed to hide a dense mat of chest hair. A hand was out-thrust to envelop Massu's in a vigorous shake.

'You remember my wife of course.'

The giant's smile swivelled towards a woman of great contrast to her husband, for where he was tall she was short and where he was built on a colossal scale she was minute; a tiny sparrow to the great bear who stood next to her.

'Of course he does, it is good to see you again.' Her voice unlike her husband's was warm and melodious but for a moment her eyes flicked sideways to where an unshaven man in a dirty coat was dividing his attention between them and the queue of passengers at the turnstile.

Massu's suitcase was picked up with ease and they joined the crowd of people who were waiting with practiced resignation to have their papers checked before they could leave the railway station. Gradually they shuffled forward and gave their papers to a bored gendarme who was about to wave them forward when the papers were snatched from his hands by the man in the dirty coat.

'What have we here?' He dragged a dirt-ingrained finger across the paper mouthing the words as he did so. 'Two locals and a stranger. I am always suspicious of strangers!' He glanced up at the giant, craning his neck to do so. 'I heard you say that this man is you cousin, is this right?

A great voice boomed over his head. 'This is my cousin Émile, the son of my father's brother.

There was a triumphant cackle from the dirty coat on hearing the words. 'Lies! I say you lie. If this was so this man and you would have the same name! I have caught three enemies of France; gendarme arrest them!'

There was a low and embarrassed rumble from Massu's new friend.

'Monsieur Inspector, I must speak to you of a delicate family matter, for it is true that this man is my cousin. My uncle, may God rest his soul, was a man of large appetites and an inclination to travel far to see those appetites fed, so this man is indeed my relative even though my uncle never…'

The words trailed off in seeming shame leaving a cynical leer on the inspector's face which only deepened as he turned to Massu. 'So, we have a proper bastard here. A no name, real-life bastard!' He pushed his long, dirty finger into Massu's chest. 'What does it feel like to be a bastard, with a whore for a mother!'

Massu had no idea what was going on here, nor how he was supposed to act, but there could be no harm in reciting his lines, nor was there any point in defending the honour of a fictitious mother.

'Monsieur Inspector, my name is Émile du Chamberlain. I travel to see my wife and family and escort them home, I stop here for only a short time before travelling on. My papers are in order.'

Massu's speech made no impression on the dirty man and his words caused a little chest to inflate with self- importance.

'I will judge if your papers are in order…bastard. So, you go to see your wife, is she a whore like your mother?'

The man was trying to goad him into the explosion of violent words which would justify an arrest. Massu was quite sure that this was the man's intent so he repeated the declaration that he was a peaceful traveller who wished only to reunite with his family. There was a further explosion of insults, attacking not only his family but his likely morals and his upbringing at which point the giant's tiny wife began to cry, first small tears which fell like drops of spring rain, then great hiccoughing sobs which racked her body.

'You are being unfair Monsieur inspector; Émile is a good man who works hard for his family. He attends Mass every Sunday and on the holy days. He wishes only to see once again his family who miss him terribly.'

There was a cough from the gendarme which was half sympathy and half warning and the dirty coated man recoiled a little and sought to defend himself. 'Madam constrain yourself I beg you. My words may have been harsh but they are said in the service of France and I can make no apology for them.'

His chest puffed out once more as he turned to Massu.

'I have decided to let you go and you may thank this good woman for my decision. Now go before I change my mind.'

With those words, the gendarme waved them through and Massu, the giant and the little sparrow found themselves on the street walking in silence until they turned a corner and the giant picked up his wife and twirled her around and around while both laughed with joy and relief.

'We have tried that little trick only once before and I am happy that it has worked again. Against a woman's tears no man can stand for long and you see how I gave him an excuse to bully you and he rose to the bait like a hungry trout forgetting his duty like a fool. The smile fell from the giant's face and he placed his wife's feet back on the ground once more.

'Bastard Milice, scum such as they have risen in France but when this war ends I will have my revenge. With these two hands I will have my revenge!'

Massu nodded, he had heard of the Milice, a paramilitary organisation made up of right-wing Frenchmen who hunted the resistance movements with guile, cunning and great cruelty. Such men had the power of the state at their fingertips and were much to be feared and he shivered at the thought of being captured by the man in the filthy coat.

The giant clapped a great hand on his shoulder. 'Do not fear my friend. That man was but a common criminal recruited into the Milice, and no local. Otherwise he would know that my uncle has no children, either true or bastards. All the same he owes me a debt for making my little Bridgette cry.

The little sparrow looked up at her husband and smiled. 'They were shed in a good cause, husband. Now we must make our guest welcome.'

They were at a block of apartments now and Massu was led into rooms which overlooked the roofs of the town of Tarbes.

The woman walked over to a framed photograph on the wall of a woman in a long dress was hung. She pressed the side of the frame. There was a muted click and the frame swung away revealing a cavity which held earphones and a Morse sender. A few seconds work with delicate fingers and the picture once more hid its secret.

A kiss was blown to the photograph 'Thank you Mamma. I have told them of your safe arrival.' She turned to her husband. 'Supper I think while I attend to making the guest room comfortable.'

Massu followed the man into the kitchen and watched the man pick up a potato and a small knife and with surprising delicacy slice it into thin chunks.

There was an embarrassed laugh from the giant as he saw Massu looking at him. 'Always I wished to cook. My wife is a good woman and as brave as ten lions but in the kitchen she is as a small child. If I did not cook then in truth we would starve and tonight in your honour I will cook the specialty of the house.'

A pan of oil was set to heat while the sliced potatoes were coated with herbs and a little garlic.

'The potato is the king of vegetables for there are many ways of cooking him, sliced or roasted, diced or mashed, take him as you will he remains king. Oh the other vegetables they have their place, but my favourite remains the potato. One day my dream is to own my own restaurant where I will serve good plain food for the working family, food that pleases the eye and delights the palette.'

He carefully glanced at the oil and then at Massu.

'I do not know your name, but you are French that much I am certain of and you have been away a long time that much I am certain of also. A sad smile crossed his face. 'You have seen much that shocked. You came from the west so perhaps you have seen the villages that are empty of many and all the untended fields? You see Milice bastards like

56

we saw today, you see a people who will not look you in the eye and the posters on every wall urging obedience. You wonder where the young men are and why all of us walk and cars and trams lie idle in the streets. You see all these things and wonder what happened to the France you left, I can see the questions in your eyes. I can tell you in one word.

'Defeat.

'Not just the defeat of armies, though God knows that is bad enough, but it is the defeat of the soul of France which you see. When we were defeated there was a rump of France left. A puppet of Berlin but we could fool ourselves that France was still there, still all that she ever was, a wayward queen among the nations. Those Frenchmen who wore black shirts before the war rejoiced that my nation would be part of the new Europe, while those who wore red were told by Moscow to keep their mouths shut.

'So, we kept our council, those of us who wore neither red or black and perhaps this was a mistake for there were many of us, far more than the red or the black. Then came the radio and we listened to a young general who told us that the old France would be resurrected even as our dear saviour was resurrected.

'At first we were glad, hearing these words, but then another Frenchman was heard and his words were also fighting words, but his words spoke of fighting not to make an old France live again but to build a new France conceived in liberty for all. Monsieur Mandel spoke of building in France right now the foundations for a new France, a different France and his words touched us both. My wife was in the market place one day and was contacted by an agent of this New France organisation.'

There was a shrug and a smile, '…and here we are.'

The smile did not hold for long. 'There is perhaps another reason why people will not look each other in the eye and it may be that you are part of that reason. We watched the Nazi legions use our roads and our railways to invade Spain. We watched them grin and smile and then we watched far fewer come back broken in defeat and we asked ourselves why such a defeat could not have happened at the hands of our armies.

'We told ourselves that many Frenchmen fought in Spain and helped defeat Hitler but when all was said and all was done the truth was that those Frenchmen fought under different flags and our shame grew. This new France Mandel speaks of must find new reasons for pride and then once more we will be able to look each other in the face.'

He looked down at the boiling oil and smiled. 'The trick is not just in the slicing, nor even in the coating but in the temperature of the oil and the timing'

The slices were plunged screaming into the oil and many glances at the clock occurred before they were released from their torment and placed in artistic formations on three plates which were carried into the room where Bridgette was tuning a soft-spoken radio.

Together they ate and listened first to the opening drum beat of Beethoven fifth symphony and then a crackling voice.

C'est la voix de la nouvelle France qui s'adresse aux Français partout dans le monde

There was a stirring rendition of the Marseillaise and then a voice told news of a war which had spread to every corner of the globe.

The Americans had beaten a Japanese task force and invaded an important island group. The judges for the trial of Franco had been sworn in. There were food riots in Lyon and women and children had been mown down by German soldiers. Moscow claimed that a Turkish aircraft had been shot down during a 'spying mission' over Soviet territory.

News near and far, designed to inform and encourage.

At last there were messages for 'our friends in France' and both the giant bear and the tiny sparrow stiffened a little in their seats.

Massu listened to the words but they made no sense to him.

What was he to make of Jean has a long moustache? The cabbages will bring forth cognac made no sense at all and Autumn winds wound my heart was no more than nonsense. On and on the words rolled, each seemingly assembled at random until almost as an afterthought the crackling voice spoke for a last time; L'arbre est vert en hiver.'

'The tree is green in winter' made as much sense to Massu as any of the other messages but its words caused excited glances to be exchanged between his companions. There was a silvery laugh from the little sparrow.

'That was very quick. You must be an important man, Monsieur. You are to leave here tonight. The messages are instructions to resistance groups all over France. Some I suspect mean nothing at all, but each group will recognise their own messages. You are the tree, Monsieur. There are four seasons and many colours. Each one in combination give different instructions, the message said both green and winter and that means that you are to be sent as soon as possible.' She turned to her husband with a trembling smile on her face. 'Promise me you will take care?'

There was no answer from the bear but he lifted her up so that her face was level was his. There were no words exchanged between them but a blind man could see the love that joined them and a tiny hand reached out and touched a stubbled cheek.

And then the moment was over, love gave way to war and a huge hand gripped Massu's coat. 'Get dressed, there is a curfew and patrols so follow me and do everything that I do.'

They followed a tortuous route down back alleys and along damp pathways and twice were forced to hide from low voices and probing beams.

Massu had the idea that they were near the railway station because he could smell smoke and soot, but in truth he was lost in a maze of streets and alleys that made no sense to a mountain born man.

His time would come, he was certain of that but for now he was a prisoner caught in the net of subterfuge and sabotage that had been flung across France.

At last they crept down a pitch-black alley way and a back gate was gently opened that led through a vegetable garden to a black painted door.

The door was ignored instead a window pane was tapped by way of enquiry.

'Papa Boule, Papa Boule, open your door!

'Papa Boule, Papa Boule, open your door!'

Three times the pane was tapped and three times was the summons issued until at last a grumbling voice was heard coming near.

'Is a man to have no peace in his own home? Cannot he sleep without every vagabond and idler disturbing him?'

The door was opened revealing a short, stocky shadow.

'Oh it's you.'

'Yes Papa, I have a package I want you to deliver.'

There was a grunt from the shadow. 'You'd best come in then.'

The door was closed behind them and they were led into what was obviously the parlour of the house, a candle was lit revealing a man in his late fifties with great bags under his eyes and a sour expression on his face.

'Now? I thought that I would not be needed until…'

'Now, Papa, it must be now, the radio said as much. Are you ready?'

There was another grunt and a shrug of shoulders. 'As much as I can be. I am due to take the 6.34 with young Henri, will that do?'

Massu's guide nodded. 'That will do nicely, in fact I was…'

'Jean-Claude what is this noise, who are these people and what are they doing in my best parlour in dirty boots?' A face wearing long grey hair in twin pigtails and holding a candle had appeared in the doorway. The face looked as if it had been woken from a deep sleep and was none too pleased with the fact.

The old man whirled round on his wife his deep-set eyes filled with concern and anger. 'Peace, woman, this is man's work and the less you know the better it is for you. How many times have I told you this? Return to our bed and I will come up shortly.'

The grey pigtails were unimpressed by this little speech and stubbornly held their ground. 'And how many times have I told you Jean-Claude Boule that I took vows before God himself to aid you in all things. For thirty-five years I have warmed your bed, darned your socks, mended your shirts, aye and bore you two fine children into the bargain. And now you seek to shame me in my own home!

'We have guests. Have you offered them coffee and why are they still standing like unwanted strangers?'

The pigtails turned to her guests. 'I am sorry Messieurs, my husband thinks that because he can drive an express train then he is allowed to be rude. Please excuse me and I will return with what poor refreshments my house can provide.'

Massu was both amused by the woman's resolve and impressed by her bravery. Twice in one night now he had seen women exhibit simple courage and it was obvious to him that the French women of the resistance were the equal of the widow he had left behind.

Papa Boule shrugged with resignation. 'What is a man to do with a woman like that? If the Milice come round then ignorance is her defence, but can I convince her of that? A more stubborn woman I have yet to meet!'

He turned to Massu eying him critically. 'I am to take you to Toulouse but it is too dangerous for you to travel by train as a passenger too often, so we hide you in plain sight. You will play the part of my fireman and shovel coal and I warn you now that I have a reputation as a good time keeper. Play me false, play the weakling and the buckle end of my belt will give you cause for much regret.

'You look solid enough, but time will tell. This is no job for weaklings and as God is my witness you will bless the hour we see the Gare du Nord. Am I clear on this matter?'

Massu agreed to do his best as the pigtailed woman entered bearing coffee and lightly toasted bread

'Too late for supper, too early for breakfast' agreed the engine driver. 'Coffee and toast will settle our stomachs and allow us to think.

'Now as to young Henri that is no problem; he always was more muscle than mind, I tell him that I do not need him as fireman for this trip and he goes away to make sad cow eyes with his latest girlfriend.' He looked at Massu and an already sour face soured a little more. 'You on the other hand are a problem.

'You are a soldier…do not try to deny it. You speak as a soldier and worse you hold yourself as a soldier. You have seen too many parade grounds to pass as a civilian. How you have managed to escape notice before now is due solely to the mercy of God.

'Well no matter we will take our chances when the time comes. And no fireman dresses as you do; that coat is far too fine and underneath you wear a suit. Holy mother of God you will stand out like a palm tree in a field of cabbages! I had thought to steal clothes more fitting to your station, but now?'

The grey pigtails stirred and placed her eyes on her husband. 'There is your spare uniform, my dear.'

Boule made an expression of dismissal. 'Bah! Look at the two of us, centimetres divide us and I do not speak only of height.' He patted a round stomach and for a moment a rare smile defeated a sour expression. 'He has not had the benefit of your cooking my dear. Even our tall friend here is envious of your apple dumplings is this not so?'

The giant gave a deep rumbling chuckle.

'Your husband speaks nothing but the truth. My one desire is to steal from you your recipe and then in truth my life will be complete, but what is it that you suggest, madame?'

There was no reply from the pigtails only a flurry of nightdress as she ran upstairs and returned bearing a short, thick leather coat, corduroy trousers, a cotton shirt and a wicker sewing basket. 'The coat is but a matter of moving the buttons and the shirt is easy also but the trousers will take much work and there is little time.'

She pointed at her husband and the giant. 'You pair get out; this young man and I have much work to do.'

Massu was then prodded and measured and remeasured once more before the old woman was satisfied and then he was commanded to sit while she worked.

Scissors sheared at her will and a needle and many metres of thread flew through cloth at her command until at last she declared herself satisfied and a red faced Massu was forced to strip and redress in front of a woman old enough to be his grandmother.

The two exiles were recalled and made admiring noises causing the old woman to blush in turn. 'It is a poor enough work I have done and I hope that no seamstress sees it, but it will pass I think.'

High leather boots, a scarf and a greasy cap complete with goggles completed Massu's transformation but Papa Boule was not satisfied and ordered Massu to walk up and down in his new clothes.

'Now you look like a fireman who has just left the parade ground, that walk will betray us both. Cannot you walk any better than that?'

Massu shrugged his shoulders; a life time in open mountain meadows had been grafted onto a soldiers training and despite his best efforts his body insisted on the familiar patterns.

Boule's wife shook her head at the sight, murmured a few words in her husband's ear, rose and returned a few moments later with two small pebbles plucked from the garden.

'Take off your boots, Monsieur', she commanded.

Massu obeyed and a single pebble was inserted into each boot. The boots were retied and once more he was ordered to walk, finding that the pebbles were uncomfortable enough to throw his feet off balance.

The second smile of the night broke out on Papa Boule's face. 'You walk like a crippled duck but at least you do not march like a soldier. You are complete now I think.'

He turned to the giant and held out his hand in farewell. 'Half an hour until dawn. You will need the last of the night to return.'

For the second time in twenty-four hours Massu was crushed to a giant chest and for the second time a giant voice rumbled in his ears. 'Jusqu'à notre prochaine rencontre, bonne chance mon ami.'

And Massu was left, disguised as an engine-drivers assistant with half his outward journey done and many kilometres still to travel and a princess still to meet.

AGAINST THE WIND

Yves Massu could no longer stride like a soldier; indeed, it was a minor miracle that he could walk at all for Papa Boule had done his best to kill him.

Massu had met many fanatics, the war had bred them by the thousand but the sour-faced man who rode the footplate was a fanatic of an entirely different family. Boule worshipped the god of speed with utter devotion and Massu was not so much his acolyte as a slave compelled to worship the same god.

There was an art to being a fireman and Massu was no artist but under Boule's direction he was turned into a machine delivering coal to the raging fire that ate fuel, grinned with white flames and demanded yet more.

Hour after aching hour Massu shovelled coal to a litany of curses each one devoted to the god and each one describing in great detail the worthlessness of Massu and the many failings of his efforts.

But at last there came a time when the litany ended and with a much-reduced fire the engine slid into marshaling yard to await its next journey.

Massu's shoulders felt as if a thousand hammers had pummeled them, his spine had promised never to forgive him while his legs consisted of little more than quivering jelly and acid filled muscle.

Surprisingly Papa Boule gave him the sour grimace which Massu had come to realise served the man as a friendly smile.

'Two minutes late. Not bad for a fool shovelling bad coal. With more practice and good coal we may have made better time.'

The grimace became even more sour. 'I have seen grown men reduced to tears after a far shorter journey, aye and taken the toe of my boot into the bargain but here we are, this is the Gare du Nord of Toulouse.

'Here is your suitcase, take the gate to your left then cross the road and take the footbridge over the canal. The Hotel L' Occitania will then be seen, you are expected and you are to wait there until contacted.'

He thrust out a grimy hand without losing his grimace.

'Au revoir et bonne chance mon ami. Remember us and if you return be sure to ask my wife to make for you some of her apple dumplings.' He patted a round stomach. 'I recommend them. Now off you go.'

And Massu walked, taking Boule's directions and all the while trailing behind him the scent of soot, coal dust and rancid sweat.

The clerk at the reception desk at the Hotel de L' Occitania was a thin-faced man who wore a shirt with a worn collar and cuffs. He looked at Massu's coal-dust covered body and hid his distaste and then had to hide it again as coal dust accompanied a signature in the registration book.

Despite his revulsion he managed to bestow a professional smile on the ragged reeking pile that hid Yves Massu. 'Merci Monsieur, room five eleven. I hope you enjoy your stay.'

An errant gust of wind blew a little of Massu's scent towards him and the professional smile wavered a little and then with grim effort rebirthed itself.

'There are showers at the end of the corridor on every floor and for a very reasonable fee the hotel provides a laundry service.'

It was a delicate hint and a less tired Massu would have grinned in appreciation at the subtlety of the clerk. Instead he merely grunted a terse farewell.

Naturally, for the Hotel de L' Occitania was in urgent need of repairs, the lift to the fifth floor refused to work and just as naturally the shower refused to provide hot water. Massu did not care. He applied soap until the water for all its coldness ran clear and then applied a rough towel to an over tired body.

A hard bed welcomed him with soft arms and he drifted off to sleep and dreamt of madmen and apple dumplings, waking only when the sound of a soft knock on his door was heard.

A soldier's habit had him instantly alert and reaching for his pistol but the sound was not repeated.

Massu's pattern of sleep had been broken and could not be remade so with a curse he rose and looked around the room then out through a window with badly cracked glass and saw only grey roofs and grey people scurrying along grey roads in the grey light that late afternoon had provided. The entire scene was somehow depressing and Massu turned away still wondering what had awoken him when he saw a folded paper had been slid under his doorway.

The soft knock had obviously been made to point him to the paper and a few short strides saw it opened revealing the message inside.

Je te verrai au chaton aveugle ce soir à huit heures.
Ton frère,
Gérard.

He had an appointment at an oddly named place only an hour from now and a life time spent as a soldier told him that time spent in reconnaissance was never wasted. He would leave now, dressed in the anonymous clothes the suitcase had contained.

The thin-faced clerk was still on duty when Massu, now free of coal dust, appeared at the desk and asked for directions to *The Blind Kitten*.

For a moment the composure of the clerk almost cracked but once more the professional smile reappeared. 'But of course, Monsieur. The place you seek is on the Rue Agathoise, no more than a short walk from here. It is a most distinctive building and impossible to miss.'

Massu left the Hotel with a hand-drawn map and the clerk's puzzling words that he hoped Massu would find all that he wished at The Blind Kitten.

A few moments walking as full night took hold brought him to a garishly painted building with every window bricked closed and an over-muscled doorman standing in front of a firmly closed door.

A withering glance and an obvious flex of muscles was bestowed on Massu and a growling voice asked if he was a member. Massu could only shake his head, and upon seeing this a great paw was thrust out. 'Twenty-five Francs.'

There was no attempt at negotiation, and seemingly no awareness that such a sum was the equivalent of three days wages for an average Frenchman, there was only the out-thrust hand.

Massu shrugged and for a moment turned his back on the doorman to open his wallet which was full of banknotes. Every one of them were forgeries of course, though very good ones, but common prudence dictated that the doorman should remain unaware just how rich Massu might appear to be.

He faced the doorman who pocketed the notes and gave a single blow to the stout door. A peephole slid open and Massu saw a single eye staring at him.

'New member.'

The door opened and Massu began to move forward but was stopped by an outstretched hand.

'No trouble…understand? No trouble or I'll hurt you.'

Secretly Massu grinned. He had killed people far tougher than this thug and it would be the work of seconds to break the out-thrust arm and tear muscles from their housings. The grin died. He would remain in character and so gave a subservient nod and walked into a barely lit interior.

He recognised The Blind Kitten for what it was the moment his eyes adjusted to the gloom for he was a man and a soldier. Such places had existed for all of history and he now realised exactly what the hotel clerk had meant about wishes being fulfilled. He took a booth by the kitchen door which gave a good view of the main door and a line of retreat if things turned ugly.

An unenthusiastic waitress in a creased uniform delivered a greasy sausage which was mostly bread and a thin beer which was mostly water.

While Massu watched the floor of the Blind Kitten fill with men. Some were obviously regular visitors who knew the waitresses well enough to flirt with them by name; other were newcomers who had summoned up courage and twenty-five francs to sate curiosity or satisfy lust.

The overhead lights dimmed while the spots on the stage brightened and a master of ceremonies with slicked back hair introduced the first act of the evening 'Mimi.'

Mimi proved to be a woman nearer forty than thirty with bleached blonde hair who proceeded to slowly undress herself with professional artistry and then, when fully naked, to invite members of the audience up on the stage to play with her breasts. For a price of course, such delights were not to be given away, but Mimi seemed a popular act, well-versed in words of encouragement in a seductive voice which was of course wholly false because she was engaged in a business transaction, no more and no less. After mining this particular seam of lust to exhaustion she left the stage, gathering up her clothes as she did so.

Mimi, proved to be no more than an introduction and the stage soon sported men and women in every combination possible and a few Massu would have sworn were impossible. To Massu they were all surprisingly un-erotic, almost mechanical in action though the crowd's cheers and the occasional muffled groan showed that he was very much in the minority.

He finished his pretend sausage and ordered another false beer, slightly bored with the proceedings but resisting the urge to look at his watch. Such an action would be out of place here and it would do no more than draw attention to himself.

He'd defended his booth with a baleful glare that put off even the bravest of men but it did not stop the woman who slid into the seat beside him. 'Buy a girl a drink?'

Massu looked at the woman; what she was and what she was selling was obvious and it was no surprise given the nature of The Blind Kitten. Still, she was an inconvenience. His contact might already be in the room and would certainly not approach him while she was with him. It would be better to get rid of her as quickly and with as little fuss as possible so he might be alone and she might find better prospects. After all the woman had a living to make.

He shook his head and smiled. 'Alas Mademoiselle, I have the inclination.' He patted his breast pocket. 'I have the cash…but sad to say I do not have the time.'

He had hoped that such a gentle rebuff would be enough but to his astonishment his little speech was greeted by a flash of very white teeth and a pleasant laugh. 'That is such a shame. Your brother Gérard had no complaints.'

Massu did his best not to laugh out loud. His contact had made her approach with great skill and no little audacity and he decided to frame his reply in a way which honoured the woman's subtlety. 'Obviously, Mademoiselle I was mistaken. My brother always had an eye for beautiful women.'

Once more he was rewarded with a flash of white teeth and a silvery laugh.

'Perhaps then it would be better if we left. I live not far from here.'

The over-muscled thug at the door bade the women farewell by name and gave Massu the benefit of a lopsided leer which he ignored even though his first impulse was to remove it tooth by tooth.

The walk, as promised was not far and brought the pair to a neatly kept flat equipped with a small kitchen, a bed and some mismatched and obviously second hand furniture.

The woman sat down on a threadbare chair and removed her high heeled shoes with a groan of relief. 'These shoes! They will be the death of me, I swear!'

She gazed up at Massu with bright green eyes set in a heart-shaped face fringed with strawberry blond hair cut so that it fell to one side in a most attractive fashion. She shrugged at a fate hidden from her and gave him a sad little smile.

'Or perhaps something else will be, that is in the hands of God.'

Her smile brightened and she moved towards the kitchen summoning forth bright blue flames which were employed in heating water. Soon there came the welcome sounds of poured water and a spoon briskly stirring against china and a face which had never quite lost its smile handed Massu a cup trailing fronds of steam into the room.

'I am sorry but this is what passes for coffee in France these days; it is warm and that is perhaps the best that can be said of it. Perhaps you are used to better?'

It was a gentle enquiry and Massu shook his head. The British had brought tea to Northern Spain and for some unfathomable reason the black leaves had taken hold, first rivalling and then surpassing coffee as the drink of choice and Massu had long since succumbed to the habit.

'I have drunk far worse Mademoiselle and it is a most excellent way to wash away the taste of a sausage who has brought disgrace to his family.'

Again, Massu's words caused the silvery laugh.

'Of all the disasters that have fallen on France perhaps the greatest is that inflicted upon her reputation as a place where food is honoured above all else. You have captured her plight with great accuracy, Monsieur…? Forgive me, but I know you only as a code word and to call you *Mr. Tree* seems a trifle formal, do you not think?'

Once again this was a gentle enquiry wrapped in great charm and Massu decided that there was little harm in bending strict protocol. Besides the woman was right, *Monsieur. Abre* did sound more than a little ridiculous so he returned her laugh with one of his own. 'My mother named me after her Uncle Yves.'

His hand was grasped in one far smaller and delicate.

'Yves, my name is Gabrielle, and for tonight you are my guest and tomorrow I will be your guide to those who will prepare you for your next journey. You will be safe here. If asked the doorman will see you only as another of my customers. Of course, he will still expect his usual fee from me.'

There was only a little bitterness in Gabrielle's voice and Massu was given a glimpse into a far different world to his own. This woman fought many wars, she fought in the court of public opinion, she fought against the risk that each buyer of her services would leave her bruised or worse, she fought for survival in world that sought only to take and never to give. Hers was a life to rent, a dream for hire by the hour or by the act. Less than a wife yet more than friend and in all this she still laughed and still held her courage high.

Massu had seen many brave women for in the twin republic's courage was not dependent on gender but this woman fought her wars alone and was all the braver for that. He was about to comment on her courage when he heard cries of pain from the street below and then the sound of footsteps, the slamming of car doors and the diminishing sound of an engine.

His look of alarm was eased by a soft hand and softer voice.

'Do not be alarmed. We are safe here. What you hear is the curfew. There are few who are allowed to avoid its restrictions; doctors, nurses, priests who must perform last rites and even then, they must have the correct papers. To be caught without them is to suffer a terrible fate; a beating certainly and then in the morning you will be hauled in front of a judge and sentenced. If lucky then the sentence will be a year or two in a labour battalion; if unlucky then enlistment in one of the French battalions that aid the Germans.' Again her laugh came with a tinge of bitterness. 'But you may console yourself with the thought that as you are being sent to be worked to death or shot in some God-forsaken land then it is French justice that has sent you there. Germany fights on many fronts and many fronts require many men, men she no longer has, so she takes from us what little we have left and forces them to fight for her. She bends our laws to her will, and what is worse sends her victims to aid her cause not in the uniform of France but in her own.

'What you heard was a thing so familiar to me that it causes me no shock but do not worry, the patrols keep to the street and you and I are safely caged in this room until the sunrise.'

Massu risked a look from behind drawn curtains. The street below was empty of light and empty of life. There was a blacker pool of darkness under an unlit street light which could be blood or just a trick played by his own eyes.

He turned away to meet Gabrielle's amusement. 'You see, Yves you are quite safe. There is only me, you and the curfew.'

There was a moment of silence and then both of them laughed and Massu realised that he was indeed a prisoner both of the curfew and of Gabrielle. To be a fatalist was an essential quality for every soldier and when there was nothing that could be done it was best to accept the situation.

He looked around his prison cell once more, familiarising himself with his surroundings. A small kitchen with a cooling kettle, two shelves with a shockingly small amount of food in in one corner, worn-out furniture consisting of two mismatched chairs, a tall wardrobe and chest of drawers with a broken handle. A bed with a small cabinet beside it lay in the middle of the room and contributed the only decoration in a room bereft of any other ornament save a vase holding a single flower placed before a photograph of a small girl.

Massu was not greatly experienced with children, especially small girls, but there was something odd about the girl who was perhaps five years old. That it was taken at a birthday party was obvious for there was a cake and the girl wore a formal dress and a paper hat but there was a curiously blank expression on the girl's face.

Massu's childhood had been one where poverty was kept at bay by hard work and birthdays were not celebrated but he believed that such a cake deserved far more than the child's apparent impassivity.

Still it seemed to be polite to mention the photograph so he pointed at the wooden frame and smiled. 'A pretty girl; she is your sister perhaps?'

There was a family likeness so this did not seem too unlikely a guess, but Gabrielle's answer surprised him.

'She is my daughter and she is dead.'

A bleak gaze met Massu's innocent words and the silvery laugh had entirely vanished to be replaced by a look of hate and despair.

'I will tell you her story, Yves, though it is not a pretty one. I was married once and I married young to a much older man who swept me off my feet with his charm and his manners. At first all was well; I was in love, my husband was a rich businessman and we lacked for nothing. Nothing apart from a child for my husband required a family.'

Gabrielle gestured to the photograph. 'My little Adele was born and at first all was well; my husband had wanted a boy but hid his disappointment well. Then as Adele grew so grew her problems. She was quick to talk yet so hard to train and the slightest swerve from the pattern of her day brought fits of temper that were truly worrying. My husband, may God punish him, blamed me for her afflictions and swore that the child was not his. Over and over he accused me of taking young lovers and called our child not a daughter but a bastard. At last he left us and sought to have our marriage annulled.

'Then came the war and all was chaos. I tried to make the best life I could but my husband's friends conspired against me and I could not find work. I had no family, no one to turn to. At last the authorities came to me and said that my little Adele must be sent to a special school in the country, a special school for special children with special doctors who would transform my child and make her whole.'

A single bitter tear ran down Gabrielle's face but she took a brave gulp of air and carried on. 'I was promised that in no more than a year, two at the most, my daughter would be returned to me and in the meantime, I was to prepare a home for her while she enjoyed fresh air and sunshine. I could visit the school and check on her progress, but it was so hard to find the money and so hard just to survive. I became what you see before you but still I longed for the day when we could be reunited.

'Twice I saw my little girl and each time she seemed a little thinner and a little more unhappy but I told myself that all was for the best and soon this bad time in our lives would be over. By denying myself and saving every centime I was able to visit a third time but my child, my little

Adele was no more. A heart attack, I was told and I was taken to a cemetery and shown a little wooden cross with my child's name burnt into it. There were many crosses there, Yves, many, many crosses and the school was empty of children. The bitch of a nurse who took me to her grave wore the badge of the Revolution Nationale and told me that she was glad my daughter was dead as she and others like her were a stain on France.'

A terrible smile appeared on Gabrielle's face.

'I prayed over my little girls grave and then left that bitch bleeding on the ground and broke my best shoes on her face.'

She took another shuddering breath and shook at the remembered images. 'But her cross, Yves, my little girls cross, it was unpainted. The bastards had murdered her and then could not be bothered to give her a decent burial. Unpainted, Yves, my child lies under an unpainted cross!'

This small detail broke the dam of Gabrielle's courage and she broke down in great wracking sobs that only subsided when Massu wrapped his arms around her and stroked her face seeking to stem the flow of tears. Clearly her courage had been born out of much sorrow, but there was little else he could do to mend it for both were warriors in a world which held much sorrow. So, he continued to hold her until she broke free and wiped her own tears, apologising for her emotion.

'I returned and joined the Forces de la Nouvelle France and help where I can as you can see, but also with information, for men are often careless with women such as I and sometimes I am sent to seduce selected men and if I may be forgiven my pride it is a rare event when I am turned down.'

Her smile returned. 'And now I think it is time that we sleep.'

Massu looked at the single bed with great alarm but there was not a shred of embarrassment on Gabrielle's face.

Nevertheless, he turned his back and heard the sounds of clothes being removed and sheets being turned down.

'Thank you, Yves. That was an unexpected kindness and now to spare you any embarrassment I will perform the same service for you.'

A quick glance showed that Gabrielle was securely covered up with her back firmly turned away from him though to his dismay he noticed that she was shaking with unsuppressed laughter.

Carefully and with a very red face, Massu undressed and positioned himself on the very edge of the bed and fell fast asleep. It was only later in the black of night that he sensed rather than saw her face only centimetres from his own and felt her hand reach out to still his lips.

'Say nothing, Yves. I am what I am, I am what you believe me to be. To others I am a substitute, a vessel into which they may pour anger or fear, but tonight I ask that you just hold me. Not as a lover but as a friend, just hold me, nothing more.'

'This is a very strange situation', Massu thought as he put his arms around her, '…the prisoner giving comfort to his jailer.' He hoped his family back in Asturias would understand. Indeed he thought they would, for each adopted child and his adopted wife had seen their share of sorrow and each had known fear and faced it in their own way even as Gabrielle was facing it now. Courage, even courage such as hers was a thing both strong and weak; it was strong towards the enemy but when forced to look inwards it could become weak unless reinforced by outside strength and that was what she was asking for now. She was not asking for the act of love, that was common enough, but for the most basic and most compassionate of acts, that of simple touch.

She nestled into his arms with murmured thanks and a single hot tear that burned Massu's skin long after it had dried and once more sleep took him until the joyful song of the kettle woke him and once more he drank burnt acorns masquerading as coffee while a breakfast of oats boiled into a mush served as breakfast.

There was no embarrassment between them now, a bed that both had shared had broken every vestige of discomfort and only joy and laughter remained. Gabrielle was even singing a country tune as she readied for the day's journey, busying herself with her hair and face

A shaving kit and a towel were laid out for him and he accepted her gracious offer of a toothbrush. It was a greatly refreshed Massu who acknowledged that he was ready for whatever the day might bring.

With a smile Gabrielle picked up her handbag and retrieved a brown-paper package from her wardrobe and guided him onto the morning streets of Toulouse.

Massu had no comparisons to make for he had no pre-war experience of the big southern city but it seemed to him that Toulouse had seen better days. Cars had been abandoned for lack of fuel and lay grey with dust at the roadside, the few trams that ran were packed inside with desperate and the hurried humanity.

The black market was in full swing and not at all concerned with evading the few indifferent gendarmes who patrolled with steady beat.

'It is the only way we can survive', said Gabrielle noticing his gaze. 'The black market and barter is our life. A single bicycle tyre can be traded for three chickens or five kilos of potatoes and you will note that the city has far fewer cats and dogs than it used to have. Fortunately, the Germans have taken many of our young men so that is fewer mouths that we have to feed. But we will walk, it is good for our figures…and besides what choice do we have?' She grinned at Massu and led him with confidence to a grand public building that reeked of the pride of a long-lost France.

Long granite steps led up to ornate doors that guarded with polished dignity a last bastion of civilization. They swung open with oiled ease and Yves and Gabrielle walked through them.

THE LIBRARY

The librarian was a figure out of a nightmare. Thinner than any stick, prim and upright, equipped with a black business jacket and black-rimmed glasses suspended on a black cord around a stiff neck. She was deep in conversation with a German soldier who needed a German-French primer.

'Why your own army cannot supply you with your own books I really do not know. Perhaps if they did then you would not be here right now bothering the good citizens of Toulouse with your ungrammatical requests.'

Massu grinned, it was obvious that the soldier was in a battle he could not win. The librarian held every weapon and obviously had no intention of lending him a magazine let alone a book.

The soldier was in mid-reply when the librarian's icy hand stopped him in mid flow. 'One moment young man. Yes, Mademoiselle. Can I help you?'

Gabrielle gave the woman her very best smile. 'Good morning, Madame. My friend and I were looking for books on early French history.'

The librarian's dark eyes did not blink. 'To study is to grow. Go to the second floor, walk forward ten paces, turn to your left and you will find the books on early French history on the bottom shelf of the last stack. I particularly recommend *An introduction to early France.* It is a very large book that perhaps your gentleman friend should carry.'

'Thank you, Madame, that is most kind of you.'

Again, the eyes did not blink nor did the librarian's expression change. 'It is no trouble at all, I assure you.' Her eyes turned to the hapless German soldier and her voice filled with ice. 'Whereas you are causing me no end of trouble. I will write to your commanding officer and I will say…'

Whatever black message a German officer was about to receive remained unknown as Massu and Gabrielle walked away with barely suppressed laughter.

'We should not laugh, Yves. Really we should not.'

Gabrielle's upturned mouth and sparkling eyes denied her words and she fought again to suppress a laugh that struggled with all its strength to escape until with a great effort she subdued it. 'Yves, all is well. I gave the code words and received the correct response. Further we have been given our instructions. All we can do now is carry them out.'

An introduction to early France indeed turned out to be a large book and one heavy with time, pages and much dust. It was obvious that so large a tome was a book designed to repel even the most studious but with a grunt Massu lifted it and placed it on a reading desk and began to idly turn the pages not knowing what to expect next. Long minutes passed and still he turned the pages not knowing how the next stage of his journey would begin. Then there was a discreet cough and he looked up to see a man in his middle years dressed in a brown work coat and equipped with a clipboard attached to a small, wheeled cart.

'Pardon me, but my name is Duparc and I am the conservator of books for this library. I noticed that your book has a damaged spine and such things if left unattended lead to further damage. I wonder, if before it leaves our care you would permit me to carry out a small repair. It would not take long I assure you.'

Gabrielle nodded and gave a brief smile. 'Of course, Monsieur. This book deserves the best of care and as I am most interested in your work, perhaps I could be allowed to see how it is carried out.'

They both followed Duparc to a small service lift and descended into the lower levels of the library where unloved books went to die and books who had been loved too much went to recover after their amours. This was Duparc's kingdom and it smelt of glue and new leather. It was filled with books in every stage of repair and much to Massu's surprise it was also the gateway to a second land.

A section of bookcase slid to one side revealing a brightly-lit room and a man and a woman who rose with smiles on their faces. The woman hugged Gabrielle while the man stood back though the smile never left his face.

Duparc to turned to Massu and introduced the couple. 'Monsieur, I would like to introduce Alexandre Lippman and Justine Lévy. Outside of these walls both would be forced to wear the yellow star and run the risk of deportation but within these walls they are what they always were; brave and true citizens of France. Madame Lévy taught dressmaking at the school of design in Nantes and Monsieur Lippman is a printer of note from our own city. Together they will ensure that you reach the Italian border in safety.'

The woman had finished hugging Gabrielle and together they opened the brown paper bag which the latter had retrieved earlier that morning from her wardrobe, revealing a green uniform with black facings, a forage cap with a death's head badge and a pistol and holster.

Lévy threw up her hands in delight. 'My dear this is perfect; you are so clever!'

The uniform showed no sign of damage. There were no holes in it and no blood stains. The uniform looked as if its previous owner had merely undressed and then forgotten to retrieve it. Massu saw a gleam of triumph in Gabrielle's eyes and immediately understood just how she had acquired the uniform. He couldn't help wondering how she had disposed of the body of her former customer.

Lévy withdrew a wallet from the uniform and handed it to Lippman who opened it with care and evident joy. 'The very latest type of identity papers. Much can be done with this. Thank you, Gabrielle.'

Gabrielle blushed her thanks and turned to go, her part in Massu's journey now over but an outstretched hand halted her progress and spun her back to face him.

'Thank you, Gabrielle. You are a brave woman and I owe you a great deal.' Massu paused, took a deep breath and then spoke in a great rush. 'When this is over, if you want I will send for you. There can be nothing between us for I have a wife and family but where I come from there is much need for people for we have suffered grievously in this war and many good men lack a woman's hand. There you may live again and raise a new family. I do not ask you to forget your little Adele but to live the life you deserve, the life you have earned.'

He ran out of breath and fumbled in his pocket, drawing out a bundle of well forged banknotes and not bothering to count them pressed them into Gabrielle's hands. 'This is for Adele. Buy her a headstone, ask a priest to bless it and say a mass in her name. It may bring some peace to her soul.'

There were no words from Gabrielle only a tiny hand touching Massu's cheek and then she was gone leaving him there to be transformed by Lévy and Lippman.

Hours later Massu was the possessor of a perfectly tailored uniform and the holder of well forged papers. He was also a new man; Hauptsturmführer Henri Mazière of the SS division Charlemagne and he was ready to undertake the last part of his journey to Italy.

Against the wind.

WEARING THE UNIFORM

The sleeve was pulled straight against Massu's wrist and Justine Lévy gave a grunt of satisfaction and pronounced herself satisfied with an afternoons work.

'Now you look the part. Your own mother would pass you on the street without so much as a second glance. I have done all that I can do. The uniform fits you far better than it ever did its owner and is its own passport for few will question it.' She laughed and clapped her hands in delight. 'You are indeed Hauptsturmführer Henri Mazière.'

Alexandre Lippman looked up from a giant magnifying glass with a smile. 'But there may be those who think that Justine's skills insufficiently guarantee your new identity and so I have given you an extra layer of defence. My camera and pen have done all that they can and I have transformed your Soldbuch and before you leave it would be as well to memorize the details.'

Massu looked at the cardboard covered book with some interest. He had seen them before of course for every German soldier carried one and he'd stripped enough corpses to be familiar with them but to see his own face staring back at him was disconcerting.

Lippman laughed at Massu's discomfort. 'I am a very good forger, although I say so myself. There are more than one set of papers in occupied France that are the work of my hands so you are not to worry. Now we need a reason for Hauptsturmführer Henri Mazière to travel to the Italian border.

'Such travel involves a journey through those parts of France conquered by Italy, and just what excuse could a member of the Charlemagne division have to travel to those parts? We thought long and hard about this question and you must thank Madame Defarge, the librarian you met at the front desk, for the solution to our problem. She has suggested that we use the situation in Italy and a weakness in our enemies here to provide you with such an excuse.'

There was a wry grin from Justine Lévy. 'You have met Madame Defarge, what did you think of her?'

Massu's first thought was the woman would not be out of place in a line of battle and would be a formidable opponent but then softened his words. 'She seemed a redoubtable woman, but perhaps a little…?'

'Bitter, Monsieur. The word you are looking for is bitter. Her husband served aboard a destroyer and was killed in battle with the Germans in northern waters while her only son was killed defending the Toulon Arsenal when the Germans treacherously broke their word and attacked the ships there. She is alone and most bitter towards the Fascists, but do not doubt that she is a most clever woman and it is she who has designed our little scheme. She is in contact with many departments of the occupation forces for her complaints flow in a poisonous stream on a daily basis. As a result, she has an extensive collection of replies and so we have examples of letterheads and signatures to choose from and from them we have concocted orders that will allow you freedom of movement.

'Also, you need transport and though the trains have served you well they are too limited an agency so we must obtain for you a vehicle and there is our first problem. A litre of gasoline in France these days is a rare thing indeed and only two organisations have access to fuel. For good reason we need you kept away from the Germans. After all, Monsieur, there may be someone who knows the real Mazière. So, we use the Milice. Not the front-line bastards but the part-timers, the clerks who guard papers, fuel and cars for a little extra cash and are willing to betray their country for temporary comfort.'

Lippman took this as his cue and laid out a collection of official looking documents on the table. 'This is Madame Defarge's ideas made solid. Now as you can see…'

All in all, it was a very intimidating uniform and it fitted the man perfectly. The forage cap was at the exact angle laid down in the dress manual with the death;s head badge burnished to a dull sheen while the jacket was adorned with more than a few medal ribbons, prominent amongst them the gold wound badge that so few gained and still lived.

The clerk let his gaze run carefully over the man who wore the uniform. He noticed the sleeve band bearing a single word that caused a silent intake of breath. Moskau. The man looked much as any other man, neither tall nor short, not broad nor thin, yet that single blood red band with the silver letters in gothic script told that this was no ordinary man.

Everyone knew the story of course how in Russia, Army Group Centre battered their way through mud and rain towards the still beating heart of Bolshevism and how they came to within a few kilometres of the Russian capitol and how the weather had overnight turned clogging mud into solid drivable ice. Their last thrust had brought them to within striking distance of Red Square itself and there was the famous photograph of the lead units of the SS advancing down a street with the spires of Saint Basil's in the far distance. A small group to be sure and one that became much smaller. The side street was the high tide mark of Army Group Centre and a bloody retreat winnowed the SS with grim efficiency leaving few indeed to wear the coveted sleeve band.

Truly the man was one in a thousand and the clerk wondered what such a god was doing here in the small hours past midnight in a small depot that the Milice had commandeered many months ago

There was a small cough and he looked up to see a face that held an expression that was half amusement and half hard duty looking down on him.

The half-hidden amusement vanished and the voice was as dark as ice. 'My name is Hauptsturmführer Henri Mazière. I will need to see your commanding officer at once.'

This was an order and one that not only fell to be obeyed but obeyed without delay, so the clerk rose up swiftly and returned with his commanding officer still rubbing the sleep out of his eyes.

Chef de Main, Roland Tarascon was not an impressive figure and being disturbed from an uncomfortable sleep at his desk had not improved his appearance but he stiffened on seeing a Hauptsturmführer of the Charlemagne division standing before him with that look of disdain on his face. He attempted to straighten rumpled clothes but the man in the impeccable uniform halted his efforts with a single wave of his hand.

'You are in charge of this depot?'

Tarascon could only nod, his power of speech wilting under the man's scornful gaze.

'And how many men under your command?'

'Four, Monsieur…Hauptsturmführer. The gatekeeper, young Hubert here and two mechanics, but they are in the garages. We are a small depot and our duty is simply to ensure that the vehicles are ready for use in the daytime. The mechanics repair what is required, Hubert attends to the paperwork while I…' Tarascon's voice trailed away for in truth he added little to the running of this little depot and had been placed here where he could do little harm other than waste time sleeping.

He looked up a little shame-faced and sure that this hero had pierced his secret but the man ignored his shame and spoke again, waving impressive looking papers under his nose.

'I have been given important orders and intend to see them carried out without delay. You also have been given orders which you will see in a moment. I am told that this depot houses vehicles without markings of any kind, is that true?'

Once more Tarascon could only give a nod which earned no reply from the Hauptsturmführer who turned on his heel and pointed a long arm at the clerk. 'You, Hubert, can you drive?'

There was a squeaked reply from Hubert which indicated that he had some driving skills and the long arm was lowered revealing a smile in which humour had no part. 'Congratulations, Hubert. This is your lucky night. You are now a temporary member of the Charlemagne Division. Outside you will find a small suitcase, take it and place it in a car of your choice. Make sure that the car is well supplied with fuel and then return here for further orders.'

Hubert hesitated for a second, his eyes darting between the man in the impressive uniform and the man still rubbing sleep from his eyes. There was a growling noise from the throat of the Hauptsturmführer at this slight uncertainty and Hubert remembered his dream of one day fighting for the new Europe. He made a decision, and ignoring an increasingly outraged Tarascon did two things. He jumped and he vanished, with old dreams of fighting Bolshevism taking new forms as he strode out of sight.

A rueful smile was turned on a red-faced Tarascon and both hands were held out in supplication. 'I owe you an apology Monsieur Tarascon. I have disturbed the good running of your depot. My only excuse is that I, like you, fight the enemies of France. My orders give me no choice and speed is required. I promised you orders and if I may follow you to your office you may read them and see that my rudeness has the excuse of a higher authority.'

A little of Tarascon's anger evaporated. If he received orders then those orders absolved him of any responsibility and his quiet life could resume so he allowed Mazière to follow him and read the orders that the Hauptsturmführer had given him. He was not aware that he was reading one of Alexandre Lippman's forgeries; the headed notepaper was perfect and the signature a familiar one but Lippman had with great care scrubbed and polished away a brief reply to one of Madam Defarge's complaints, replacing it with an equally brief instruction to give Hauptsturmführer Mazière anything he required due to a matter of grave national urgency."

Mazière had moved behind Tarascon's chair and laid a friendly hand on his shoulder as he was reading the orders. It was obvious that the Hauptsturmführer was part of some large event and that even the half-forgotten leader of a small depot could rise if he played his part well. He began to form in his mind the words which would gain the favour of such a man when the surface of his desk rose up and blackness reached out and seized him.

Yves Massu harboured a good deal of frustration. It was true he now once more wore the uniform of a soldier, albeit an enemy one, but for the past few days he had not been the master of his own destiny. His life had been ruled by sea captains and madmen, amateur chefs, taciturn railway-men, thugs and prostitutes, librarians and dress makers. He had been a parcel passed from hand to hand, the hands were owned by brave men and women. That was true but for a man used to mountain air the procession of keepers was irksome and his irritation grew and possibly it was that longing for independence which guided his actions now.

His hand left Tarascon's shoulder and placed itself behind the head of the Chef du Main and before the man could react, slammed Tarascon's head down onto the desk. Every ounce of Massu's frustration was in that push and the man's forehead and nose hit solid wood with a satisfying crunch.

Instantly the great blood vessels in Tarascon's brain and eyes burst open and the delicate membranes that held each in place split and ruptured. He was already dying as Massu wrapped a long-looped telephone cord around a throat that was taking its last gasping breaths.

Massu pulled on the chord until he was certain that every vestige of life had left his victim's body and then with great delicacy replaced the phone back in its place and swiftly walked over to the window and looked down on the ill-lit courtyard below. Young Hubert had obviously chosen his car and was very sensibly equipping it with cans of fuel and tools.

Massu grunted with satisfaction; the boy was obviously armed with a fund of common sense and it was a true shame that it was employed in such a cause. Still it gave him a few moments in which to make his next moves.

Madame Defarge's plan was to sow doubt and confusion in the ranks of the Milice with the false orders which Lippman had so painfully forged. The orders would gain him both entry to the depot and a vehicle. Eventually they would be found to be false and when order was restored Massu would be long gone.

And yet Massu was a senior sergeant in the Asturian Guards Regiment; the night was dark and the gatekeeper easily avoided. Only two people knew of his arrival and one of them was now long past caring. A new plan had formed in his head and as soon as it had appeared Chef du Main Tarascon was a dead man. There was a far better way of giving him time to escape and the death of the depot chief was just the beginning.

A slammed car door in the courtyard below gave notice that Hubert had completed his preparations and would soon retrace his steps. Massu returned to Tarascon's still bleeding body, lifted the broken head by its hair and removed the forged orders which he disposed of behind a file cabinet.

Obligingly Tarascon continued to pour a mixture of blood and spinal fluid over the table and within moments there was no trace that the paper had ever existed.

He was only just in time; footsteps announced the imminent return of Hubert and Massu sprang to the doorway and began a conversation with the cooling body of Roland Tarascon thanking him for his cooperation and promising a glowing report to his superiors. The broken head of the depot chief made no reply of course and he firmly closed the door, turning to face Hubert and adopting once more the persona of Hauptsturmführer Mazière.

'All is ready?'

'Yes, Monsieur. I have chosen our best car and I am ready to drive you wherever you wish.'

There was a moment of pretended thought before Massu replied. 'Our journey will be a long one. You will need a change of clothes. Your first task will be to arrange that. Then I will give you further directions.'

Hubert had chosen an anonymous Citroen sedan as his vehicle of choice and as the car drove up to the guard-house Massu cursed and pretended to drop a notebook, ducking down to retrieve it so that the guard saw only a familiar face as the big Citroen drove through the gates. Hauptsturmführer Mazière was now a ghost with the only witness to his existence sitting beside him gripping the steering wheel and driving towards the undistinguished block of flats where Hubert lived.

With orders not to delay Hubert vanished into the flats and Massu began the next part of his plan. A sharp knife stripped away insulation and cut deep into copper and Hubert returned to find the Hauptsturmführer sitting exactly where he had left him.

Naturally the car refused to start and Hubert received a long and invective-filled description of his personal failings. He could see his long-held desire to serve France in the uniform of the S.S retreating faster every second and he looked around wildly seeking an escape from this crisis.

'A car, Monsieur. We can steal...take a car!'

The street, like many in Toulouse, was littered with cars abandoned for lack of fuel and Hubert ran to one which seemed less dust-covered than most and a moment's work saw a dry fuel tank receive life-giving fuel poured from the cans so carefully filled. Fortunately, there was just enough charge left in the battery to energise the fuel pump which sucked fuel and threw it into dry cylinders who ate it as though long-starved. Massu watched as the rest of the cans were emptied into the new car and then refilled with fuel syphoned from the one he had killed.

Hubert had proved a most resourceful companion, but for all his ingenuity he had been no more than a puppet. Now, when Tarascon's body was discovered, they would find Hubert missing and what would be more natural than to suspect him as the killer? A search of his home would find missing clothes and a car which would not work. Even the most stupid of policemen would assume Hubert's guilt and believe he had left on panicked feet. The stolen car would not be missed out of so many and in occupied France witnesses were few and tended to see little and remember even less.

Hubert was praised for his quick thinking and drove east never knowing that he had an appointment with the guillotine.

Massu smiled and Hubert gave back the grin of one who had successfully shown an initiative which would bring great reward.

And so began the journey of Massu and Hubert and while both the Milice and the local Gendarmerie looked in every corner of the city they drove north and east.

Gabrielle bought a tombstone with the money Massu gave her and had her child reburied with every ceremony the priest could provide and while the words were being said she cried tears of joy and release and wondered what kind of new life awaited her at war's end.

Papa Boule drove the return train back to his home and a wife who baked the world's best apple dumplings and refused to share the recipe with a giant of a man who dreamed of opening a little restaurant of his own.

And all the time Massu and Hubert drove north and east, always taking the back roads, resting at wayside inns paid for with bank notes that were the work of master forgers in faraway Gijon.

Ever North and ever east...with Hubert sharing his dreams of working for a new Europe where Teuton and Gaul fought the dragon of international Bolshevism and of a strong France newly reordered, purged of undesirables where everyone had a pre-ordained place.

Eastwards now through the Gorge of Tarn where the river ran blue with joy and the rocks were white with age while on a coastline far away an old man mumbled nonsense to the gulls and waited for orders that would shine lights red and white and a young man with few words mourned the loss of a mother and a people.

And still Massu and Hubert travelled, down now to the roads that circled around Avignon where the popes of old lived and on to the village.

The village was one of hundreds they had passed through, each a few houses clustered round a church that marked a man's life with a weekly beat, fields with fat sheep and fatter cows, a fountain where every Monday the women gathered to wash the family clothes and gossip.

They were gentle lives and ones Massu had no intention of disturbing. His route was carefully planned to avoid much contact with anyone at all. Small depots either of Milice or occupation troops were plundered for fuel with Hubert's obvious pride at being the driver of such an important man combined with the uniform of a combat veteran enough to overawe the sergeants and over-age lieutenants who ran the small garrisons and Massu signed for fuel with the florid signature of Hauptsturmführer Mazière.

But at the village they were stopped by a hasty barricade thrown across the single road that lead both into and out of the village and a Milice corporal who saluted as he saw the man the car was carrying.

'I'm sorry sir but the village is closed, we are conducting anti-partisan operations.'

Massu looked at the corporal with disbelief. There were no mountains nearby to provide rocky hideouts, no woods to provide shelter. For a partisan or a saboteur, the land was not only barren but profitless. Long experience in Spain showed that whatever activity there was would be at a very low level indeed and that a man of Mazière's experience would know this so he raised an eyebrow and looked pointedly at his watch, and then pointed at the flat, sheep-filled fields that were still dew-wet from the night's chill.

'I have orders which allow no delay and whatever problems you are having with the local livestock are no concern of mine. I insist you allow me to pass through.'

The corporal reddened at the words but looked at the uniform and the impatient face of the man who wore it and decided a corporal's stripes were not proof against such displeasure and allowed the barricade to be opened, knowing that higher ranks were in the village and it was far better that they argue with the forceful Hauptsturmführer.

He received a very stiff salute for his pains as the car drove off and he returned to gazing at the sheep and dreaming of turning one of them into a tasty meal, for rations had become somewhat thin of late.

Massu tried not to let his tension show as Hubert drove slowly into the village. He had not planned for this meeting. His idea was to move a swiftly as possible using as many minor and obscure roads as possible, depending on bluff to get him through, but now an obscure village had thrown every plan into doubt.

A thin man with a hatchet face stood on the steps of the village fountain waving a pistol and giving orders to men who were pulling people out of houses and pushing them towards the church; on seeing a strange car approach he jumped down and walked over to the slowing car, gesturing to Hubert to stop.

Massu noticed that the man did this without asking for assistance nor delegating the task. Whoever this man was, he was no Roland Tarascon, but a man who would be far harder to fool. Still the game had begun and must be played to the end so he fixed on his face an expression which indicated boredom and impatience and got out of the car when asked to do so.

Massu's stolen uniform which so far had proven irresistible was given only a grudging glance of admiration by the thin man and it was only the papers so carefully forged by Lippman which overcame the doubts of what Massu saw was a mind both shrewd and suspicious.

'What brings you to this village, Monsieur? Surely this is a most indirect route. In a few kilometres, you will be in the Italian zone and so beyond my jurisdiction.'

Massu gave a carefully orchestrated shrug which mixed exasperation with irritation at being questioned.

'My orders give me discretion as to which route I take. Do not question my orders.'

There was still skepticism on the thin man's face and Massu began to feel the situation unravelling just as he had feared so he allowed his expression to soften a little and gestured to the man to withdraw from the crowds of people being pushed towards the church.

'Monsieur, I must ask for your help and also for your discretion.' Massu took a deep breath and tried to look a little reluctant. 'You speak of this route being unusual and this village being so near the Italian zone. There is a reason for both, a reason even my driver knows nothing of and must never know.'

He paused again as if doubting whether to speak further.

Then slowly as if each word had been dragged from his throat. 'It may be that France will once more regain what she has lost to Italy. It may be that Berlin has decided that France and not Rome would make a better ally and it may be that some of us have been tasked with deciding the paths that will lead to the regaining what has been lost.'

The eyes of the thin man opened wide and Massu prayed that he had judged the man correctly as a mix of self-confidence and ambition combined with a burning hatred of Italy's ruthless seizing of French land in 1940. He hoped that the man would decide to take the hook dangled before him, wanting to believe what his heart had long yearned for and if a great event was to take place in these lands then that such a tide would raise an ambitious man high indeed.

Massu could only hope and as he hoped fear's icy fingers gripped his heart watching the thoughts run across the thin man's face. It would be so easy for caution to win out over hope and dull duty to conquer ambition and if those forces won out then his mission would end here today on the borders of a portion of conquered France.

Finally, the man's mouth opened and shattered sentences poured forth.

'The Italians gone? And here, this is where…? When, how?'

The icy fingers released their grip a little though Massu could still feel their presence and so resisted the urge to grin in relief. Instead he seemed to regret the breaking of a vow.

'Monsieur I beg of you not so loud. I cannot say what I am forbidden to say, but know that great change is coming. Italy as you know is unstable and in great need of correction and where better to look for such reform than those who have transformed France?'

Just as Massu hoped, soaring ambition flared in the man's eyes; a resurgent France would call many men to her colours and those men would need leaders. The bait had been swallowed and while it was being digested, he would make good his escape.

But it was not to be. The flicker died, a calculating smile taking its place and an invitation was given to see just how this small corner of France was ruled. There was no evading the invitation. The bait had indeed been swallowed but its digestion followed a route that Massu could not have anticipated for he had acquired a new friend who saw in him a sure pathway way to promotion. There could be no escape; to refuse would be to reawaken suspicion and so Massu and Hubert were led by the still smiling man through empty streets to the church.

The great doors were opened with a crash and a wave of fear rolled through every pew and the priest's words from high up on the pulpit stuttered and died for a moment until with a look of disdain to the intruders they re-birthed themselves, filling the space and drowning out the clatter of boots that walked up the aisle

For a moment Massu looked up into the face of the priest and felt shame. There was no fear in the priest's eyes, only contempt for those who would threaten his flock.

Massu had no use for the Church; in Spain it had shown itself to be a tool of evil and no friend of the common man but he could recognise courage when he saw it and priest or no priest the man who read from the gilt-edged book was a man he could respect and yet there was nothing he could do but see out the awful pantomime that the morning had become.

He was led into the vestry where he had been promised that he would see saboteurs and enemies of France, the truth was a little different. Two boys, aged perhaps thirteen or fourteen sat bloodied and wide-eyed with fear at one side of the room with a squat man equipped with a three-day stubble and a length of rubber hose standing to one side.

The thin man grunted with satisfaction and strode over to a table and picked up a large open tin filled with a thick yellow grease and thrust it under Massu's nose.

Massu had been brought up in the country and recognised it instantly as sheep grease. When the sheep were shorn the fleeces were boiled and the grease was extracted, for it had a thousand uses. Thick, tenacious, proof against any weather there were few households that did not have tins of the grease ready for use but he failed to see how this common item had brought down the wrath of the Milice.

The thin man gave Massu a sardonic grin and gestured to the boys. 'Nothing in this area escapes me, Monsieur, nothing at all. Four kilometres from here is a railway line and twice now grease has been smeared over the tracks causing much disruption. This morning I laid a trap and caught these two wretches in the very act of sabotage!'

Massu could see the scene very clearly; the great driving wheels of the locomotive would find no purchase on the greased rails and presumably another engine would have to be called from the depot to extract the stalled locomotive. Both the rails and the engine would have to be cleaned and he knew from past experience just how hard a task that was. This was not the work of an organised band but had all the hallmarks of a boyhood prank and he could imagine the boys watching from a distance trying to hold in their laughter.

A partisan band would cause far more damage and would certainly not tarry long enough to get caught so he had no doubt that the boys would spend some time in prison and would suffer greatly but no lives had been lost by their actions. They had lost blood and a few teeth but they were young and would recover.

He gave words of praise to the thin man and to the squat man with the rubber hose who both swelled a little with pride while the two boys shrank at this sudden attention. It was all he could do; he had given the men the honey of approval and he hoped it would be enough to send him on his way.

'They are enemies of France. We should shoot them.' The words came from behind him and were spoken by Hubert who was looking at the boys with undisguised loathing. 'They were caught in the very act of sabotage and the law allows no exemption for age. We should take them outside and shoot them!'

Massu looked at Hubert and realised he had misjudged the man and the situation. Hubert was an enthusiastic disciple of the ideology that had allowed the Milice to form. That much he understood but he had underestimated the man's wish to join the Charlemagne division. Hubert by adopting a ruthless attitude hoped to impress a man who could help fulfill his desires. Worse yet the thin man was raising no protests at Hubert's outburst, obviously not wishing to appear weak in front of a Hauptsturmführer who had hinted that great opportunities lay in front of him.

Justine Lévy had said the uniform he wore was its own passport, that deference would be owed to it and now he understood exactly what she meant. As Hauptsturmführer Mazière he had authority here. The uniform and the thin man's obvious ambition gave him that authority but any attempt to interfere would look unusual and would undo all that he achieved this morning. His deception had been all too successful and had trapped him in a tragedy where he must play the part of a dedicated soldier committed to the cause.

He was committed and there was nothing he could do.

The fate of each boy lay in his hands and there was nothing he could do.

His mind turned and turned, seeking an excuse, any reason to spare the boy's but each path each plea for mercy would involve questions, paperwork and the waste of precious, precious time.

There was nothing he could do.

Nothing.

He thought of all those who had aided him. From mad old men to bitter librarians; all had risked their lives and the lives of those around them so that he may be here at this place and this time. He wished that they could be here to give their wisdom but they were not. Only Yves Massu was here, a man caught in a masquerade turned deadly.

He could hear Hubert's heavy breath behind him and he turned once more, hoping that there had been a change of heart that would allow him to act with mercy, but he was assailed only by expectant breaths, short and fast and a curious glaze to Hubert's eyes.

There was no hope hiding in those eyes and there was nothing more he could do.

Nothing.

The two boys were dragged to their feet and pushed through the door crying and with legs paralyzed by fear.

He heard a long dead Judas laugh with understanding as they were tied to chairs in the village square and heard the keening sounds of women trying to express a grief that words could never speak.

This was his fault.

His.

His guilt and his shame.

The priest gave hurried last rites and then harsh orders cut through the morning air. The chairs fell and hot blood spilled onto cold cobblestones.

A childhood joke had turned deadly and it was his fault.

His.

He was the catalyst, the gunpowder trail that caused morning deaths.

And there was nothing he could do.

Nothing.

His guilt was plain.

His guilt was overwhelming.

There was nothing he could do.

Nothing.

The priest walked over to him and looked at him with pity and that was worst of all for the pity cut like a fiery blade. Better by far to face hate, for hate was an old enemy and easily battled, but against compassion he had no answer. The priest saw only the uniform and not the man who hid behind it and there was no way to tell him that the clothes he wore were no more than an actor's drabs soon to be discarded. For the sake of his mission he must endure an undeserved mercy and the agony it would bring and a small part of him welcomed the pain as a penance.

He heard the thin man's voice as if from a distance and he remembered he was an actor and must assume an actor's face.

'As you can see, Monsieur, should you come this way again you will find your path a peaceful one. There can be no question of disturbance while I rule here.'

The words were a subtle plea for approval and Massu the actor made the right noises, mechanically shook the out-thrust hand, and then, with a curt order to Hubert, made his farewells to the thin man and the grieving village.

Hubert's eyes shone and his mouth was full of excited words but a savage gesture ensured that the mouth remained empty and the only words spoken in the car were those of Massu giving directions.

They came to the border of Italian controlled France and Massu was once more prepared to be an actor but an unkempt guard barely gave them a glance and they drove through the darkening day and on to a small patch of manicured wilderness with a murmuring mountain-fed stream and trees whispering in the late evening breeze. A children's playground, some picnic tables and a small brick building which served as a convenience for the passing traveller completed the scene and Massu gave orders which caused the car to pull into a small gravel-filled area in front of the convenience.

Hubert, as Massu had hoped got out to use the convenience, closing the door behind him.

Before the door had fully closed, Massu had opened the small suitcase brought from Toulouse, retrieved what he was looking for and sprinted for the convenience. The door opened easily at his touch and Massu stepped from behind it, pressed the barrel of a small pistol under Hubert's chin and pulled the trigger. A bright spray of red and grey erupted from the top of Hubert's head and he fell back onto the dirty brown tiles of the convenience.

Massu watched confused legs twitch for a moment and then stop.

The pistol was wiped clean and placed next to Hubert's body and the scene looked at first glance like a suicide.

Whether the body would be linked to a murder in Toulouse was not his concern, though the thought of Hubert being considered both a murderer and a suicide did give him a moment of joy but in either case Hubert had played his part and had left the stage.

In truth Massu had considered leaving Hubert bound and gagged and trying to explain just how a mystery French Hauptsturmführer had both appeared and vanished in the course of a few days but Hubert's actions in the village had decided his fate and went partway to quieting the loud voices of his conscience.

The hated uniform was disposed of under layers of last autumn's leaves and cold stream water washed away Hubert's blood. The suitcase gave up civilian clothes and as arranged leaning against the back wall of the convenience was a bicycle which transported him away from a stolen car, a murdered Hubert and best of all the hated Hauptsturmführer Mazière.

The last stage of Massu's outward journey was beginning.

His new host was a wiry, fox-like man who had a fund of tales that told of a life lived well. His dining room was filled with photographs of the man standing next to minor politicians, artists and stars of stage and screen. The photographs were evidence enough, but a lifetime's habit made the man less than reticent about his achievements.

'I was the best of guides, Monsieur. If you wished to fish then I knew the places where the trout gathered. Hunting also, for the secret spots were well known to me. In the winter I watched the snow fill the lower slopes and I took parties up to ski and attended to their every need. Yes, I was the best of guides, but the war ruined everything and now I have nothing. Now I am not a guide, I am a smuggler. For a price I walk the paths over the border and I carry papers or small packets. I never ask, Monsieur, for it has been made plain to me that to ask would be very bad for my health, but I pride myself that I have never failed to deliver what has been entrusted to me.

'Now I am to carry you over the border. The way will be difficult and you are no small packet and I wonder if I should not have asked for a larger price.'

Massu realised that this man was only to be trusted so far, he was not interested in causes only cash but still self-interest was a powerful motivator and he could only hope that despite the protests sufficient cash had been paid. The best he could do was to express sympathy and remember to keep a wary set of eyes in his head as a precaution against treachery.

Nevertheless, the man was as good as his word; his house lay at the base of the mountains and was well-equipped with everything needed and soon Massu was furnished with stout, steel-rimmed boots and clothes proof against the cold. An ash-hafted ice axe was placed in his hand and stout hempen rope slung over his shoulder. A rucksack filled with tools and dried food completed his outfit and while an old moon threw stolen sunlight on the land the two men began their climb.

Massu had always loved the mountains and one by one the old senses came back and familiar scenes reappeared.

The sweet smell of snow pouring down from the mountain tops.

The soft clinking sound as pebbles fell under his feet.

The shadows, sharp and black.

But most of all the air that filled his lungs with bubbles white and pure.

Unused since time began this was his air, both free and precious and he almost laughed at the simple joy of it.

His guide never noticed the suppressed laughter, content as he was with thoughts of cash and of happy times that would reappear at war's end.

And so, they climbed, following cold streams that ran over ice-rimmed rocks and higher yet to where the air burned hot lungs and cold fingers ached. This was Massu's home and though the rocks were new-seen they were old friends and welcomed him.

Three cold wavering suns were born and sank redly into the rocks before they came to an abandoned shepherd's hut that sat overlooking a narrow valley filled with yellow grass growing between great boulders.

'This valley leads to your destination. I will wait here two days and no more. If after that time you do not arrive then may God help you for I will not. Good luck my friend.'

Massu looked down onto the valley. A great eagle slid sideways in the commanding air.

The bird was free.

And now so was he.

Against the wind.

FROM THE MOUNTAINS

Yves Massu was a cautious man when caution was called for so he waited for his fox-like guide to disappear back down the track and out of sight. The man was no more than a paid agent and such a man could easily barter Massu's freedom to a higher bidder for temporary gain. There would be vengeance for such an act of course, but that would be of little help to him or his mission. So, he waited for the cold moon to sink and the night-hunting eagle to seek rest and only then after he had scanned every rock and crevice did he move forward.

There was a road that ran along the valley floor but he avoided it, looking instead for the dark paths that ran twisting along steep boulder pitted flanks and walking slowly lest loose rocks fall and alert the evil minded.

All night he walked with careful feet below him and coronets of stars above him until morning painted knife-edged shadows from high mountain tops onto the small hamlet below.

For a moment Massu was overcome with nostalgia for this was his childhood made real once more. Before the war, before there was even a rumour of war, a mountain village very like this one was his home and he could with ease recognise Italian versions of the local baker and the doctor with a well-worn path to the waiting room. He watched as sleepy housewives came to never-locked doorways and began their morning rituals of cleaning and dusting. All this was as familiar in his eyes as the scars on his hands but it was not chattering housewives or doctor's surgeries he wished to see but a far different sight.

He scanned his eyes across the houses, his memories telling him what to look for, though in truth the building was not very hard to find being a little larger than most and within comfortable walking distance of the church.

Massu grinned at the sight. The building's occupant was the last link in the chain that would lead him to the Princess.

He patted the pistol which lived under his arm.

The last link, and this time he, Sergeant Yves Massu would be in charge.

For a midday morning, mass attendance had been gratifyingly large thought Father Domenico. Of course, the present political situation may have had something to do with the large number of filled pews; wars and uncertainties made people more aware of the presence of God and his mercy. As a replacement for old Father Ignacio there had been a certain reserve towards him from some members and he hoped that this morning's numbers showed that his campaign of gentle good humour was at last bearing fruit.

A man, even a priest as young as he could only hope, hope and trust to God…and his superiors, for Father Domenico had not been sent to an obscure mountain parish just to listen to the confessions of shopkeepers and their wives, nor just to minister to the woman who had fled to the small palace which long ago had placed itself at the head of the valley. He was a man sent on a mission, a man with but a single purpose, a purpose that suited him well.

There was a streak of ambition in him as well as intelligence, wit and charm which a wise church had harnessed. The seminary had seen these talents polished and it was Cardinal Montini himself who had recruited him to his office where he had yet to prove himself. This place was his chance…if he was careful.

If he was careful, then the visions he had of becoming Bishop Domenico or even Cardinal Domenico could become reality. But first, before those first rungs could be climbed, he must be patient and endure a life of semi-exile while waiting for an event which might never happen.

The garden gate squeaked on rusty hinges as he opened it and he reminded himself for the thousandth time to apply a little oil but knowing that by the time the aged body of Mrs. Sozzani opened the door the thought would be gone from his mind.

The face of Mrs. Sozzani could never in her long years have ever been described as pretty and Domenico half suspected that the late Mr. Sozzani had taken himself off to death without regret as the face was rumoured to hold a bitter tongue.

Still she was an adequate housekeeper who had served generations of priests and he saw no reason to put himself to the trouble of exchanging her for a newer and prettier model.

The face that greeted him at the door though was enough to bring the possibility of change far more forward than he thought. The long, lined face of his housekeeper seemed to have gained extra furrows which served only to accent the dark anger in her eyes.

'You've a visitor', she said without the customary greeting. 'Pushed past me without so much as *Good morning* or saying who he is or what he wants.'

Her indignation grew as she recounted the events. 'Didn't take off his boots or his coat, trailed dirt and mud all through the hallway and into the parlour and sat down in front of the fire as if he owned the place and then waved me away as if I was a person of no account whatsoever. So, who is he and what is he doing here, that is what I want to know! You should send for the police or Stefano the blacksmith and have him thrown out.'

She had nearly run out of both words and indignation but had enough of both left to utter the final damning words. 'Sitting in front of the fire with muddy boots, the very idea!'

Domenico thought fast, his housekeeper had a bitter tongue which was also far more oiled than the gate hinges. He had no doubt that by lunchtime the village would not only know that he had a visitor but would be the willing recipient of Mrs. Sozzani's considerable ire.

'Well it is a cold day, Mrs. Sozzani and it's only natural that a cold man would seek warmth and are we not instructed by our Lord himself to comfort the stranger?'

He took a deep breath, knowing that he was about to lie and hoping that a lie told in a good cause would be forgiven more readily than a lie told in a bad one.

'The truth is that this is all my fault. My visitor is an old friend returned from the wars where he suffered very badly. He has come to me for absolution and spiritual comfort, though I did not expect him so soon which is why I did not inform you. Please accept my apologies and his also for I am sure that he meant no insult and sought only the warmth of your hearth and the cooling balms of religion.'

A silent prayer for forgiveness was sent while the gaunt features of the housekeeper softened into what a kind person would say was one of acceptance and an unkind person would say was grudging submission. Either way it made little difference; she now had a tale which could be converted into the coins of gossip and more importantly he was free to meet a long-awaited visitor.

He made yet more apologies but he could see that Mrs. Sozzani was almost dancing in her urge to spread her tales of woe and long-lost friends so it was an easy task to send her away and walk through the open door of the parlour.

On such a cold day the door would normally be shut, but his visitor obviously had no intention of being surprised, an idea reinforced by the sight of a pistol that was held so it pointed directly at the doorway. The pistol did not waver nor did the voice which ordered him to slowly sit and not make any moves which might be thought threatening.

His visitor was older than him by perhaps ten years, but those ten years had obviously been a hard ten years for his eyes were black pinpoints that showed neither pity for victims to come nor remorse for victims past.

For a moment the man looked at him and a tremor of fear ran through the priest for the eyes did not leave him and the pistol still pointed an open mouth at his stomach.

'You are very young to be a priest.'

The man's Italian was a little stilted and the accent was a little hard to place. Still a conversation had been started and it would be rude not to reply so he slowly opened his hands and put on his face a smile which acknowledged the truth of the man's words. 'Very young and so very expendable. If mistakes are made then they can be placed at the feet of youthful enthusiasm. I know my place you see.'

There was a grunt from the chair and the gun was lifted until a half-closed eye looked along the barrel and into his face.

'Disposable priests are no new thing to me. I've seen them beaten from towns by the dozen, so know this; betray me, even think of betraying me and you will meet your God with six good holes in you.' The eyes hardened until their blackness filled the room and overwhelmed Domenico's smile and swamped his outstretched hands. 'Do we understand each other?'

There could only be one answer. 'We do.'

The gun was lowered and one by one the hairs on the priest's neck flattened and his bladder ceased sending urgent signals to a thoroughly frightened mind. There was no doubt that this was a very dangerous man, which was perhaps just as well but dangerous or not he must build a bridge between them so the smile returned to his face and his hands once more became emblems of peaceful intent.

'I am Father Domenico of the Papal Secretariat of State. I was told to expect an Allied agent but no more than that. You speak Italian very well but are not Italian I think?'

There was a short laugh from the man which held no humour at all. 'I am Sergeant Yves Massu of the Second Guards Regiment of the Asturian Republic, I was born in the French mountains. As for my speaking Italian, I have interrogated many Italian prisoners and have always found that my fists convince even the most reluctant to become excellent teachers.'

Domenico shuddered. Massu's regiment was well-known as one filled with men and women who hated fascism and as an organisation that combined passionate hatred with war skills and guile; while the Asturians themselves, disgusted with the support the Church had given Franco, had expelled every last priest from their lands. Yet Massu had said he was French and perhaps that was a way to build a bridge between them.

'So, you are French, Sergeant. How long is it since you attended Mass? I could take your confession and…'

Massu spat on the floor between them and Domenico watched his bridge burn to ashes as cold words came from an angry mouth. 'I do not need your blessings, priest! In France the Church taught obedience and fear of communism and in Spain the church blessed the bombs that fell on the very people who looked to it for protection.'

Another packet of saliva joined the first as Massu poured words on hot ashes.

'I am not French, I am Asturian! I swore the oath to defend what was right when your pope was taking tea with Mussolini! I fought, my wife fought, my children fought…and fought when the Church turned its back on us. And now you need us to rescue you! Well here I am, but keep your blessings as I do not need them! You and your kind are not brave, you are only self -serving. Well I serve Asturias and you had better remember that if you wish to remain healthy.'

Domenico looked at the smoking pile of ashes which was his first attempt at bridge building and decided to change his approach.

'I am sorry to hear of your suffering, Myself...well I am sorry to hear that you have suffered. You mentioned a wife and children? Your wife is a communist also?'

A little of Massu's blackness retreated in an explosive laugh. 'You listen too much to your own propaganda, priest. Socialism, communism are no more than labels to frighten children. In Spain now there are many widows and even more orphans. I married a widow and together we adopted two children and a grandmother with no one to care for her. This we do because it is the right thing to do. A man should have a family, a wife should have children to love and grandmothers should spoil grandchildren. It is the nature of things.'

Domenico noticed that Massu's eyes softened when he spoke of his family and decided that this bridge would perhaps be more proof against fire than the first. 'Then I will say a Mass and ask our Lord to bless your children. If you deny my blessing surely you cannot refuse it for your children?'

He waited for another explosive rejection, but got instead a short laugh and a wry grin. 'Both my children had killed their first German before their tenth birthday. Do you think your blessings are proof against that?'

Secretly Domenico was appalled, he had heard tales of the hard-edged war waged in Spain but to hear it from the lips of one who had been there was worse than reading reports in the peaceful offices of the Vatican. Still this bridge had survived and it was time to take the first steps across it.

'I cannot say, Sergeant. All I know is that the mercy of God is infinite and that he sees into every heart, especially those of children. Tonight I will say a special Mass and ask him to extend his protection to your children and thank him for sending them to new parents who have offered them their own love and protection.'

The bridge trembled a little but did not collapse under his feet and Massu waved grudging acceptance. 'As you wish, though I tell you now that such things hold very little value to my little ones who still keep sharp knives under hard pillows.'

Massu had taken the first grudging steps from his side of the bridge but he still held a gun and Domenico realised that the next and final steps would have to be taken by him.

'I have had breakfast but Mrs. Sozzani will have made coffee and a light meal for me in the kitchen. It is a little early for lunch, but you must be hungry after your journey?

For the first time Massu admitted to a human failing and the kitchen soon saw fresh baked bread and yellow butter being washed down by thick Italian coffee while between bites Massu studied the priest.

There was little to see; a black clerical dress covered the body while a pair of emerald green eyes which returned his gaze while giving nothing back in return.

He had long since decided he did not like the priest and hoped that his display of anger and the pistol he held had been enough to intimidate the man but realised that the lesson had been ill-learnt and that somewhere inside the man was a deep wellspring of confidence and the warnings he had given would soon wear off. With luck that time would come after the man had completed his part in the mission for after that he would not care. The words had been spoken once and one less priest in the world would make little difference.

The green eyes stared back at him and then blinked in defeat and Massu secretly grinned. He would not begin a conversation knowing that to ask questions made him a petitioner. Better by far to remain silent, let the gun in his hand speak for him and allow the priest to break the silence.

Domenico gazed at the gun which gazed back at him with a grinning black mouth. The stranger never let go of it and ate with one hand, never for a moment letting go of the pistol and never for a moment breaking his eyes away from his own.

The sight was un-nerving, like a foretaste of Judgement Day. The Sergeant was assessing him and might at any moment consign him to the fiery pit.

He gave a last look at the pistol and admitted defeat. 'You can put the gun away, Sergeant. We are allies, you have nothing to fear from me, I have my mission which is to aid you in meeting the princess.'

The pistol slowly disappeared returning to its home in a holster that lived under Massu's left shoulder while Domenico gave a short thanks to a merciful God and prayed that his next words would not cause its reappearance. 'You come just in time, Sergeant. The situation in Italy is very grave. Mussolini has been arrested by his own Fascist Grand Council.

Massu jerked his head up at the news. 'So, Italy has surrendered?'

Domenico shrugged, wondering how to convey a complicated situation. 'Yes…and no. A new Fascist government was formed under Count Ciano which promised Berlin that the Pact of Steel was as strong as ever while seeking an armistice with the Allies. Alas for the Count the Germans moved even more troops into our northern cities while the Allies called upon the Italian people to reject their new leaders and rise up in rebellion.' There was another shrug from the priest that joined with a sad smile. 'Alas I can only report that no such rebellion has taken place, instead we fight each other while the Gestapo makes arrests and the Wehrmacht puts every Italian soldier it can find in prison camps. The Holy Father is prepared to add his power to seek a solution to bring peace but without a leader that day seems very far off. We need a leader that has a place in every Italian heart, a leader that loves Italy and is both brave and wise and we had hoped that…'

'Princess Marie will pull your irons from the fire, cause an angel of peace to descend from heaven who will give the Pope absolution for the many sins he has committed and everyone lives happily ever after.' Massu's voice was cold and sneering, though Domenico noticed that this time, mercifully he refrained from spitting on Mrs. Sozzani's clean kitchen floor. 'I know all this, priest. I was told this before I left. Alas for her the price she asks for her help is far more that will be paid. She either accepts what can be paid or she and Italy can rot. That is my message to her.'

He paused and gave Domenico a grin that had not a single ounce of warmth in it.

'And you know what priest? I don't care ether way. My orders give me wide discretion. She says no? Then I disappear like a puff of smoke and find my own way home.'

He patted his shoulder holster like a man would pat a favourite dog. 'After tidying up a few loose ends of course, like priests who may give up far too much information.'

Domenico gulped and tore his eyes away from an implacable face, his ambition and dreams of advancement dying before Massu's cold grin. Now he had an even greater motivation…that of simple survival. His fate rested in the hands of a soldier who did not care about his life and a foreign-born princess who had fled from her family and had ambitions of her own.

The coffee cup was put down with a clatter which would have had Mrs. Sozzani dancing with rage at the abuse and Massu rose, giving a last regretful look at the warming fire.

'We go and meet your Princess.'

'Now? It is customary to make an appointment; the princess is not used to receiving…'

Massu's grin had disappeared and Domenico's objections withered away before the dark glare which had replaced it.

'Now, priest. We walk, the exercise will do you good, and no tricks, we are just old friends taking the morning air.'

There was no waiting for an answer only the opening of a door and a finger that beckoned Domenico into a future he no longer controlled.

THE PRINCESS

A lesser man would have been overawed by the hunting trophies, the paintings, the marble floors and the gilt-laden furniture of the palace of Sarre, but Yves Massu had hunted men and did not know the difference between a Degas and a Davinci while a chair was a thing of utility that all the gilt in the world would not change, although Princess Marie, he had to admit, was beautiful or would be beautiful if it was not for the furrowed brow and lips which had thinned in anger.

She sat in a chair which had only the very minimum of gilt while Domenico and Massu stood before her and listened to her displeasure. Massu had delivered the Allies response to her demands and it seemed that the answer was not to her liking and she hissed out her anger.

'My co-operation rested upon my brother being rescued from Nazi imprisonment and the Allies guaranteeing that the Italian monarchy will rule after the war and now you tell me that your masters refuse to risk a single soldier to aid the highest blood in Belgium and that the fate of my husband's family rests in the hands of the Italian people! Tell me Sergeant just what incentives do you offer now? And you, Father, do you still urge my compliance, even though such an act would place my brother, the king of Belgium in deadly peril? How do I live with my conscience if acts of mine cause his death? Will God forgive me for the sin of Cain?'

Domenico looked towards Massu who shrugged his shoulders and gave a brief smile while his hand fluttered up towards his shoulder where hidden under his tunic lay a gun which could end every one of his ambitions in a single barking retort. He gulped and painted a sympathetic smile on his face while summoning up every ounce of persuasion.

'Your Royal Highness, the feelings you express do you great credit. I know that the Italian people have taken you into their hearts and I cannot believe they will turn their backs on you. Your good works amongst the poor and the injured are too well known for your fears to be realised. I am certain also that the Germans will see that your brother the king is of more use to them unharmed and cannot be held responsible for any actions of yours. There can be no sin in doing your duty as best you can, God sees every thought and if your heart is pure then your soul remains unstained. I speak here not just as a priest, not just as your confessor nor even as a mortal man, but as the mouthpiece of His Holiness the Pope, the vicar of Christ. He asks that you do your duty to God, to your faith, to the Italian people and to your very soul. He points you along a narrow path and asks in the name of Christ the redeemer that you take up your cross and bear it for the good of all.'

The princess waved a dismissive hand.

'A pretty speech, Father; yet would not the same words be better given to my Father in Law, the king who has taken refuge with the Germans? Or perhaps you should send them to my husband, the prince who has forced me into exile here while he wears a uniform he never earned and wears medals he never deserved. The same husband who shakes like a leaf in the wind and cries unhappy tears onto the shoulders of his lovers. Perhaps the Allies are right; perhaps the Italian people should decide our fate and with such fine examples of the monarchy set before them they may well reject us.'

A shade of resignation crossed her face, mating with the anger and making a pretty face far too ugly though for a tiny moment of time Massu thought her eyes registered something else, some other emotion almost as if she was speaking words in a play. The moment passed and her bitter speech continued.

'I have tried, Father, truly I have tried and yet against the wind that blows through my adopted homeland my words have been truly powerless. Surely it is better to wait out the war in comfort with my children around me and accept my fate. The sergeant has delivered his message and my pleas have been rejected. Perhaps, sergeant you can take my message back and say that I will abide here until the end.'

At first Massu did not answer, but looked around the room until his eyes fixed upon a small chair that seemed to have undergone several operations by cabinet makers who believed that no surface should remain uncarved or un-cushioned. He shrugged and dragged it over, sitting down and crossing one leg over the other, knowing that this was a breach of good manners and not caring at all.

He looked the princess in the eye and spoke a single sentence.

'He was wrong.'

The words hung in the air and Massu sat unmoving in the chair until the princess could no longer restrain her curiosity. 'Who was wrong?'

'Private Deschamps was wrong. Private Deschamps was a corporal in the Chasseurs Ardennais; fought his way across Belgium and got a boat down to Spain and joined the Second Guards. The man was a genius with a rifle…and he was wrong. He said that the old king, your father would never have surrendered and maybe he was right about that, but he said that Belgium made a bad bargain when they married you off to Italy because you had bigger balls than your brother and you would have made a better monarch, one at least as good as your father and maybe better.

'But he was wrong, because all I'm hearing from you is that life is too hard, too difficult. That to me doesn't sound like someone with balls, that sounds like someone who has given up, well lady that's your concern, I'll take your message back and you can sit here and rot.

'It seems to me as if you want power without risk and without duty. You want your brother rescued so that you can play with a clean conscience.' He paused and for a moment Domenico was sure he was about to spit on the floor again but Massu contented himself with raising his voice, almost shouting at the woman who sat before him 'What about the poor bastards who will die helping your brother. Did you ever think of them, of their families? You want the Allies to give you pledges when those pledges may have to be backed up with blood but you don't care about the men who will die just to keep a crown on your head. So Deschamps was wrong, lady, dead wrong. You do not have the courage to lead. You are not worth risking my life for, nor the lives of others.'

He rose from the chair and gripped Domenico's arm dragging the priest towards the door and a fate already foretold. There was no resisting such a grip and visions of a future life that was not to be passed in front of the young priest's eyes. He was already saying prayers that he hoped would fortify his soul when God or fate intervened.

'Sergeant, wait!'

The grip relaxed by just a fraction and the blood began to flow again in Domenico's arm.

'What do you want, lady?'

'A soldier of the Chasseurs said I could lead. Does he still believe it?'

An expression of sorrow passed across Massu's face. 'Hard to tell. He lies in a cold grave half-way up a mountain. Being good with a rifle doesn't help when you're being bombed by Dorniers. He was a good comrade and a brave one.'

'I'm sorry, sergeant.'

'So am I.'

'But he believed in me and you don't?'

Massu released Domenico and turned to fully face the princess.

'You're scared, you think I don't see that? You see danger and risk around every corner and it seems impossible to think that there is a way out. Deschamps said you were like your father. You think your father never knew fear when the Kaiser marched over the border? Do you think he wasn't sick to his stomach? But what did he do? He put on his uniform and fought, that's what he did; didn't ask questions, didn't make demands, just fought. But Deschamps was wrong. You don't have your father's balls, because having balls means being scared and then doing the right thing anyway.'

There was a moment of silence and Domenico had used Massu's angry words to place a little distance between him and the sergeant when the princess spoke again.

'Father Domenico, you claim to speak on behalf of our Holy Father. Those are brave words and I now put you to the test. My children claim refuge in the Holy See and the personal protection of the Pope. Will such sanctuary be given?'

Domenico could only nod. 'The Holy Father will welcome your children and extend all the power of the Church over them, but we are many kilometres from Rome, how do you propose to travel such a long distance?'

There was no reply to the question only a thin smile as the princess turned to Massu.

'And to you, Sergeant I make an offer. Let us see if a sergeant of the Asturian Guards has the courage you think I lack. Your orders are to take me back over the mountains and into Spain where I am to become the mouthpiece of the Allies in their mission to make the Italian people rise up against the Fascists. You are right Sergeant, I am scared of such a fate and so I choose another one, but my choosing needs your bravery and now I ask if you have the courage to disobey and to do what is right. I will place myself at the disposal of the Italian people but I will do so without travelling to distant lands to become a puppet of London or Washington. My father was his own man and when danger threatened, he shared a trench and withstood bullets with the meanest of his subjects and I can do no more than that, but like my father I do so as my own person. Do you have the balls to follow me Sergeant Massu?'

Massu realised he had been trapped by his own words just as the priest had been trapped by his. That flash of eyes he had seen when the princess had made her protests had been the glint of a hunter.

'What do you suggest, lady?'

For the first time a genuine smile lit up the woman's face.

'What I suggest, sergeant is that all of us travel south to Rome, deliver my children into the hands of the Church while gathering support along the way. Then once my children are safe, we turn our full attention to removing every last drop of Fascism from the lands of Italy and so you will fulfil your mission of using my voice and the crown I wear to help my adopted land. However, in order to achieve that I will need the assistance of a capable man such as yourself.'

'Fuck!'

The British had not only introduced tea drinking into Northern Spain but had introduced their own forms of profanity and Massu, like many others had taken up both with enthusiasm and as the word seemed to fit the situation, he repeated it several more times.

The smile never abated while Massu vented his frustration and then was replaced with a far more serious expression. 'Sergeant I never had any real hopes that my brother could be rescued and in war they are few certainties about anything, but you can be certain that I hate the Fascists just as much as you do. I have prayed very hard to God to send me a sign that he has not turned his face from me and from Italy and I believe that in you he has sent me that sign. I tested you and you did not fail me. Your hatred of the enemy runs as deep as mine and now I beg for your aid for without it I shall surely fail.'

Massu thought of swearing again and then thought of spitting and then after rejecting both actions as useless tried to think of reasons why the woman's idea was the madness he knew it to be.

'Lady, Rome is a long way from here and every kilometre is covered in Germans. I was supposed to smuggle you back with help and now you ask me to escort you along a new route without help. Besides which, my orders were to escort you back to Spain or leave you here, not take you on some wild journey that could end up with you being captured and me being shot. The whole idea is mad!'

The princess nodded, understanding the man's frustration yet seeing in him a pathfinder whose reluctance must be overcome.

'I ask a lot of you, sergeant, I know this, but we will not be alone. There is a communist partisan band no more than twenty kilometres from here. They have offered to help in any way they can and there will be others I am sure.'

There was a muted explosion of protest from Father Domenico at this news and Massu turned an unsympathetic grin on him. 'What's wrong, priest? Aren't communists also the children of God, or are your prayers just for those who attend Mass?' Or maybe you are worried that the communists will treat you the way we treated your kind in Asturias?'

He turned to the Princess and now he had to decide if he wished to be caught. His orders gave him the option of abandoning the mission at any time but said nothing about altering the mission. Still he was a senior sergeant in the Second Guards Regiment and every member of that regiment was expected to exercise some discretion, besides which he was more than half certain that the fox-faced man that had guided him to the border would betray him on the return journey.

For a moment the images of Papa Boule and Gabrielle came to Massu's mind. He had been safe in their hands and would be safe again, for even if he was betrayed any trap would be easily evaded...if he was alone. That was the key, a single man could move swiftly whereas a man with burdens would undoubtably be caught and undoubtably shot.

He stared into the pleading face of the princess. 'You had this planned from the start didn't you, lady?'

'No, sergeant, I had hopes but when I saw you I saw that my prayers had been answered...and if, as I hope we are to be companions I should tell you that the proper form of address for a princess of Italy is *Your Royal Highness* and not *lady*.'

This was too much for Massu, who once more spat on the floor declaring that such words would never pass his lips and to his surprise the woman burst into laughter.

'I will never convince you sergeant, will I? So, I offer you a bargain, escort me south and I will allow you to call me by my given name if by the same token I can call you Yves.'

Massu looked at the princess, seeing the hope in the woman's eyes and knowing that is was very likely that he would regret this moment if he lived which seemed an unlikely prospect indeed but he had been a soldier for a long time and the experience had made him fatalist enough to know when his flank had been turned and when it was time to accept a temporary defeat.

'I am a madman' he said, '…that much is certain, but as you wish. If I can't convince you to be sensible then perhaps I can keep you alive for a little longer, but always remember that I lead and you follow.'

Princess Marie stepped down off her chair and gently touched Massu's weathered cheek. 'Thank you, Yves. You hold us all in your hands and I know you will not let us down. In Rome you will gain your freedom and I will fulfil my destiny.'

Massu could only shrug his shoulders at the touch but he could sense an irritating wave of triumph coming from the man who stood a little distance away

He turned to Father Domenico seeing again the light of unruly ambition on the man's face. 'You were going to say a mass for my children, priest. Say one for yourself…you will need it, and remember I always keep my promises. Any betrayal, any hesitation and it will be a sorry day for you.'

The slight smile that vanished from the priest's face and was replaced by one of abject contrition did nothing to erase the disquiet that ran through him. It would be a long road to Rome and every metre of it would bring danger and trouble.

There was only one word that could be used to describe his feelings and he used it again with even greater volume and even Marie's laughter did not help.

Sergeant Massu had been many things in his life; soldier, assassin, spy and finally husband but now he was about to undertake a new career, that of bodyguard to a princess and her children with only a pacifist priest to aid him…and a last realisation.

It was too late to turn back.

AFTERMATH OF REVENGE

The morning sun had dried the blood on Georgiou's sleeve long before they had placed the last boulder on the body of his brother. They did this in silence, each man lost in his thoughts, picking the rocks which hid the body until the cairn resembled a tumbled rockfall from the white limestone cliff face.

They moved quickly for the rising smoke from a burning truck must soon bring investigation and there was no time for more than a few hurried words over the grave.

They returned to a village of frightened but determined people; they too had seen the smoke rise lazily in the morning air and knew it to be a sign of evil portent. Already children had been gathered by anxious mothers who wondered just how much of a hard-won household they could carry.

Only the old men remained calm for their future was fixed and plain to see. They still sat under the tree and Dodd wondered if they had moved at all from yesterday but realised that age had indeed brought wisdom and they had seen that fate was fate and was better met in comfort than in wasteful agitation.

He walked up to the oldest of the men, clasped his hands and promised that if he survived his beloved granddaughter would have a husband and a protector. The words were in English, but the old man seemed to understand and smiled.

There was no time now; bundles were grasped, babes clung to mothers arms and the village emptied leaving only the old men and their memories of long ago.

Georgiou waved a last farewell and turned to Dodd.

'The people will take the goat paths to the hills and hide until it is safe to return. I have said goodbye to my mother and told the priest what I have done.' A sad grimace crossed his face and he looked again at his brother's blood which stained his clothes. 'Matt, I fear that my sins are too great even for God to forgive and perhaps the Devil will at last claim me.'

Dodd could make no reply to this, his religious upbringing was limited to dry sermons in dusty churches with the odd more recent visit from

Army Padres and he lacked the words which would give absolution. Besides he had come to the truth that in war there were only the quick and the dead; the dead had no regrets and the living had no time for regrets…if they wished to carry on living.

There was only one remedy for regret and that had its foundations in soldiering. Movement and the solving of problems were cures which had served him well in the past and he did not doubt that they would serve Georgiou in the present and would perhaps go a long way to removing the mark of Cain.

His decision was easy to make, almost instinctive; to stay in the village would be to join their fates to the fate of the old men, so he ignored the anguish in his friend's voice and asked a simple question.

'Which way?'

Georgiou shook himself like a dog shaking off the effects of unwelcome rain and pointed up towards.

'Up, we too will take the goat paths.'

He shook himself once more and stared at the village as if trying to commit it to memory, then with a great sigh he turned and pushed a weary body up the hill which stood guardian over the houses.

Dodd followed in silence, for there was little that he could say and it seemed best to allow his friend to find his own salvation as he climbed under the hot sun.

As a pathfinder Georgiou was unerring, and an hour's climb brought them to a clear pool which sprang from a great cleft in the rockface. Dodd's mouth, which had become increasingly dry as the ascent steepened, welcomed the sight and he bent down scooping the cool water in great gulps only stopping when his thirst fell away.

He stood to find a hesitant smile on Georgiou's face.

'Did you enjoy the water, my friend? This is a holy place, those who wish to bear healthy children come here to pray and bathe in its waters. My cousin, who all thought barren came here and was delivered of twins though it is very true that nothing could persuade her to make a second journey. Here we will fill up our canteens, but we cannot stay.'

Dodd nodded, to stay near running water was to invite disaster; the noise of an enemy patrol would be masked by its burbling laughter.

Both men hefted full canteens onto waiting shoulders and forced aching legs up and away from the sacred pool through the undergrowth to the very summit of the hill which gave them a good view of the village and the road that led to it.

Two trucks ran along it raising clouds of dust that hung in the air undisturbed by any breath of wind.

Dodd and Georgiou could not hear them for the distance was too great but they watched as the trucks drew up in the village square and tiny figures descended from them and walked over to the old men who had not moved from when Dodd had waved goodbye.

They could not hear the questions nor feel the blows but could only watch as a helpless audience while the play was performed. They watched as a silent pistol spoke and a figure fell, watched as silent fists hit silent mouths as rifle butts broke men old in years and resolute in defiance and watched as empty houses were searched in vain.

At last there were only broken figures lying dead on the ground and the first plumes of smoke from burning buildings.

They had known it was coming but it was still hard to see and Dodd watched as the tears rolled down Georgiou's face.

'Kill and destroy, it is all those bastards know. My uncles, the priest gave their lives as they promised to do. I too can make promises. I promise to find those bastards and make them suffer as my uncles suffered.' He wiped the tears from his face with a rough hand. 'This I promise, Matt. My luck has brought ill fortune to those I love and it is up to me to make amends. Look, even now the bastards seek new blood!'

The trucks had refilled and were now leaving the burning village following the path taken by the fleeing villagers and a moment of panic gripped Dodd.

'Athanasia, your mother, they will be safe?'

Georgiou could only shrug.

'As safe as God makes them for they are in his hands now. They will take the hidden paths to safety but I believe the old men have bought them time with their lives and surely God would not see such courage go unrewarded. We can do no more than pray and seek revenge. Come it is time to seek shelter and I know a place where we will be safe.'

Georgiou's place of refuge was a cave well hidden by myrtle trees that fought an eternal war with tribes of wild goats. A high roof was pierced by several openings which let dapples of light fall onto a rubbled floor. It was the ideal place to hide, but there was only one drawback. There was little point in having a secure bastion if it became merely a place in which to starve.

Dodd emptied a small rucksack onto the cave floor; ammunition, soap, a small mirror and a razor fell out followed by four packets of dried bread, a bar of chocolate and two tins of pressed meat. They would, with care make a few meals, none of them particularly filling, none of them particularly large.

There was an unspoken question on his lips as he watched Georgiou's bag surrender an equally poor harvest and a small paper bag which he threw into Dodd's lap.

Dodd opened the bag to find two braided cords flaring out from a central pouch. There seemed to be no clear purpose to the device and Georgiou laughed at his puzzled expression.

'You wish to know what it is you have in your hands?

Georgiou's laugh grew louder as Dodd's puzzled expression deepened.

'What you have there my friend is breakfast and dinner. Before I left the village, I asked my mother if she had kept the toys of my childhood. Naturally my mother had kept many things from those years and this was one. Tonight we sleep without fire and eat our meals cold for the Germans will have patrols out and it is best that we take every precaution but tomorrow I will show you how a toy will give better food than ever came from a can.'

The dapples of light had begun to fade now and Dodd ate American meat with an obscure genealogy and drank holy water that he hoped would not result in twins. He had taken the first watch and was sleeping when dawn came to the cave and when Georgiou's hand woke him.

'It is time for breakfast my friend. Come and I will show you how Greek boys hunt.

They both walked out into the sunshine with Georgiou carrying his strange toy and gathering pebbles as he did so.

The wild goats had already started their breakfast, chewing on stubborn Myrtle bushes. They started at the sight of the two men but then resumed eating, though keeping a wary eye on the intruders.

Georgiou placed a stone in the leather pouch and began whirling the device around his head, then with a curious underhand motion caused the stone to fly towards the goats. It struck one with bone-breaking force causing a piteous bleat and the stampede of its companions.

A contented smile broke out on Georgiou's face, and he carefully wrapped up his childhood toy. 'I do not know what you would call this in English, but it throws the stone very fast and the good Father once told me that long ago a young boy killed a giant with such a toy. The Father told few lies though I hunted goats not giants. It kills silently and this is important when there are those who would hear the sound of gunshots. I picked a nice fat one, though I was aiming for its head. I am sadly out of practice, Matt.'

A swift knife ended the goat's suffering and a few moments work reduced it to manageable chunks one of which made an enjoyable breakfast over a brushwood fire in the centre of the cave.

'I cannot hope to cook as my mother cooks, Matt, for there are herbs she uses which add flavour, but we will not starve and that is surely a good thing.' He wiped his sleeve across a greasy mouth and stretched out like a contented cat. 'You never had time to sample my mother's cooking for there was no time but at your wedding feast there will be such meat and to spare. Goat and lamb such as you have never tasted and dancing, Matt; we Greeks love to dance. You are the most fortunate of men for as the world knows, Greek women are the best that God has made and my cousin has a gentle soul.

Dodd was surprised. 'Athanasia is your cousin?

Georgiou grinned, 'But of course, you will also be my cousin, Matt. In Greece family is a very big thing, which is why...'

The words trailed away as he gazed sadly at the knife which had cut into his brother's heart and there was a moment's silence which filled the cave and seemed to make even the bright flames of the cooking fire recoil in sympathy. At last he stood and kicked the fire to death and a smile, every inch of which was forced, slowly reappeared on his face.

'The dead are sad enough. Better I think to remember my brother as he was and to hope that in heaven his sins are forgotten. Now if we are to kill this general it is best that I show you where the devil lives.'

Only memories of a boyhood's wanderlust guided Georgiou, but the memories did not deceive and a scrambling morning's trek across narrow valleys brought them to a high escarpment which overlooked a twisting and much wider valley populated by only two houses. The houses were set very far apart, almost at opposite ends of the valley; one house much smaller than the other lay where the main road began, while the other had gathered to itself a collection of temporary wooden huts along with a vehicle park.

'When my mother was a young girl this was a great scandal', Georgiou explained. 'A man from Athens built the large house and installed a young mistress thinking to deceive his wife with a house so far away. Alas for him and alas for the young girl the wife found out their secret and built the smaller house and from there she would scream at them as they drove past. At long last she tired of this amusement and walked down the valley and shot the mistress and her husband.'

Dodd was intrigued with this tale of ancient tragedy. 'What happened then?'

It was almost impossible to shrug from a prone position but Georgiou did his best. 'I do not know. The tale ends there, but I do know that these are places of ill omen and thus it is fitting that they house the bastards but I do not see how two men such as ourselves could hope to attempt such a deed as you have proposed.'

Dodd could only agree. The two houses were fortified with barbed wire and gun emplacements; there was a guard house at each end of the twisting road connecting them and the area was patrolled by leashed dogs and alert sentries.

The situation seemed impossible and all that day and for the next three days they studied the valley looking for any sign of weakness. Each night they returned to the cave, drank holy water and ate slaughtered goat.

On the fifth day they made their way back to the high lookout point and looked at a familiar routine. Before the sun had risen too fully a motor bike complete with side car left the large house and drove at a sedate pace towards the smaller house where it waited for a large black car complete with general's pennant to drive through the guard house. From there it escorted the car to the large house which Dodd guessed was the actual headquarters, the much smaller house serving as a residence for General Bräuer.

Each time Dodd looked not at the tiny convoy but at his watch while Georgiou cursed Bräuer as a lazy coward who would not take healthy exercise and was too terrified to walk half a kilometre of good Greek road without an armed escort. Dodd ignored the words while the hands of his watch measured precious moments.

Each day Georgiou's frustration grew and his curses grew more inventive while Dodd thought and planned. There was a chance, scant seconds to fill long moments of effort, but a chance all the same.

Later that night he took a long swallow of water that all but guaranteed conception, looked at his companion and fought to keep the excitement out of his voice.

'Tell me, Lucky, just how good are you with your toy?'

Electric stars gazed down on the burnt village, gazed down on scattered corpses and charred wood. In time the corpses would be buried with honour and charred wood replaced with the newly hewn. Other days, other stars would witness those acts but tonight's stars witnessed the opening lines of a most dangerous play. Weapons were checked and checked again, water bottles were brim filled and a last mouthful of unfortunate goat provided a hasty meal.

There would be no time later so hands were clasped in these last moments of peace and then the night-time walk along now familiar paths to the appointed place where many days had been spent watching and there they waited, each man lost in his thoughts, each man counting down the hours.

The pre-dawn light was a royal purple that slowly vanquished stars curious to see what the day's new hours would bring. They were doomed to disappointment. All they saw before the dawn removed them was Matthew Dodd and Georgiou Papanastasiou clambering down the hill side to walk across the road and hide amongst the trees which threw long shadows towards the west.

It was a gamble; from their vantage point Dodd could not see all of the road but he could see the tops of many tall trees and more importantly he could hear. Each day he could hear the engine of the motorbike and side car being throttled back and that could only mean one thing. A bend existed, possibly a sharp bend and the rider was obviously of the opinion that that such a place was better taken slowly. Even better the rider and the side car would be moving from bright morning sunshine into the black shadows cast by the trees. That small portion of road was concealed from both guard houses for a few precious yards and whoever drove along it vanished from human sight.

It wasn't much, just a series of guesses, assumptions that could lead to disaster but the alternative was to abandon the effort and that Dodd was not willing to do.

So far fortune had favoured them; the trees hid the rising sun and deep black images of leaves and branches lay on the road. Better yet a great bulwark of limestone had thrust itself out of the earth and the road had very sensibly decided to go around it in a sharp bend.

A nod to Georgiou was all it took. He stepped out already swinging his sling in a fast fluid motion.

The rider had already throttled back, the practice of many days guiding his hands. Soon his duty would be complete and there would be coffee in the mess - poor quality that was true but hot and that was the main thing. He was only just aware of his companion making a noise that expressed puzzlement when Georgiou's pebble hit him in the chest.

It wasn't a large pebble, only a few grams, but it held a great deal of energy in those few grams and it had been aimed by a man who had recently been polishing a boyhood game into a deadly skill. It ignored cloth, scorned flesh and drove a broken rib into a heart only just beginning to panic. It was an extraordinarily lucky shot sent by a man renowned for his luck.

The rider never knew that of course; never had time to realise that. He had only time for an instinctive pull on a brake lever that stalled his machine and last thoughts of family, of a mother buried under rubble, of a brother entombed in an iron coffin, miles under the Atlantic, and of a gentle father who guarded stubborn civilians in a castle by a river. Then last thoughts faded and like vanished stars never saw the play continue. He never saw Dodd run out and reach towards his companion with a left hand that lifted a terrified head up while a right hand punched savagely forward breaking a throat so that lungs starved.

In a way this was a mercy for he was spared the indignity of seeing himself and his companion stripped and his machine restarted by alien murderers who had killed and hoped to kill again.

Later, much later, at a castle set above a sluggish river, a man much worn by war would weep bitter tears and would be consoled by men and women who the state called enemies but he called friends. But this he did not know and would never know. Instead sightless eyes gazed at a departing motorbike and side car.

And a play that must continue.

So far, they had been lucky, or perhaps his guesses had been devastatingly accurate. It didn't matter. Georgiou had stepped out into the shadows and flung a stone that left far too quickly to be seen. Again, that did not matter, only the effect mattered; the motorbike came to a halt giving him time to play his part.

Long ago he had been taught by men whose profession it was to kill with sure silence. Over and over he had practiced until he received grudging smiles as a reward.

Instinct guided him.

Left hand on the forehead and push quickly before defensive arms could act.

Draw back the right arm as far back as nature allowed.

Clench the fist.

Strike hard, strike sure.

Feel the enemy's larynx fail under the blow and watch skin pale and eyes open wide into unanswered pleading.

And then it was over, this act of the play was ended and costumes must be changed.

Dodd and Papanastasiou switched from Greek peasants to temporary members of the Wehrmacht, pulling dark goggles over faces that had slain their former owners, kick-started the stolen machine and drove carefully up to the guard-house outside the General's residence.

It still was a matter of Papanastasiou's luck and Dodd's judgment. He was careful not to drive too slowly and to cling to the righthand side of the road, even when the play threatened to turn into a tragedy. They were late, of course they were late; it took time to kill and time to strip corpses and restart a stalled engine. They were only moments late but it was enough to earn a savage rebuke from the guard sergeant who pointed to a car already waiting.

Dodd swallowed hard and thought quickly, pointing to a fuel tank and mimicking the actions of refilling it. He hoped this was enough to soften the sergeant's wrath, but the sergeant had other ideas and began to stride towards him with the obvious intent of delivering the sort of rebuke that sergeants have ever given to those set below them. He was but a few yards from Dodd and in the very act of drawing breath for the first of many angry words when the car signalled its impatience.

The sergeant just had time to wave an angry finger before turning and shouting orders that saw the guardhouse barrier lifted and the car move forward.

Dodds could hear Lucky mutter under his breath but whether those words were curses born of fright or grateful prayers he could not tell and there was no time to ask. He swung the handle bars around and began to lead the car back along the road. There was no time to look back only time to exercise more judgement for he must draw ahead of the car to gain precious seconds; not too fast lest suspicion be aroused but enough to give time to do what was needed.

The drive to the bend seemed to take decades and the urge to push the throttle forwards almost irresistible but at last they reached the point where just for a moment the car and its escort lost sight of each other and it was time for the next act in the play.

The car rounded the corner to find their escort not leading the way but halted and blocking the road.

The driver was obviously a man of great perception and no little courage. Realising that there could be no retreat, realising that he faced not friends but enemies in stolen costumes he did the only thing that firm resolution would allow. With a roar of his engine he threw the car forward, determined to crush Dodd's machine under its tyres.

It was a brave move and one that Georgiou was determined to prevent, already he had swung out the side-car's machine gun and it chattered out its objections in a stream of bullets that crazed glass and drew white sparks from black paintwork. Nearer and nearer came the car, the stream of bullets seeming to have no effect on its accelerating bulk while beneath stolen goggles Georgiou's mouth was fixed in a grim line.

Nearer and nearer, the machine gun's roar loud, the bullets striking armoured glass which collapsed into silent shards with Dodd only seconds away from flinging his machine away from the path of the charging beast.

Nearer and nearer until with a scream of tortured engine the beast collapsed onto shattered tyres.

Dodd was still not satisfied and with a quick twist on the throttle he allowed Georgiou to fire at point blank range into the flank of the car, hammering a last stream of bullets the length of the vehicle.

Then for a brief second there was silence all the more voiceless after the loud noise of death until Dodd became aware of other sounds.

He heard Georgiou's ragged breathing, harsh and laboured, the crackling of a cooling gun barrel and the soft hiss of steam escaping a devastated radiator and then he heard the sound of an alarm warning a newly-roused garrison.

The sound broke the spell and his hand ripped open the door the reveal the inside of a demented butcher's shop.

General Bräuer had never been a handsome man and several bullets had not improved his appearance. His driver, hands still gripping the wheel, gazed with cold eyes through a shattered windscreen, but there wasn't time to do more than glance at the blood splattered interior of the car or smell the odours of fresh death.

He reached into the car and pulled a gore-soaked briefcase from Bräuer's cooling fingers and with a roar of stolen engine accelerated away from the wreckage.

They were only just in time. The strident klaxon had done its work well; trucks were filling with armed men and motorbikes that were twins to the one they rode were already leaving their compound, an excited sergeant pointing with an excited arm.

Those that knew Dodd best knew that he combined a natural stubbornness with a strong fear of captivity. These two attributes had seen him trek the length of France with an exiled French politician in tow and they served him well now as he turned off the road and up the hill with several angry Germans in hot pursuit not far behind.

As he knew very well the Germans were very good engineers and made excellent motorbikes but there came a time when even the most superb engineering was unable to handle the steepening sides of a Greek hillside and the motorbike was abandoned with Dodd and Papanastasiou hoping that where wheels had failed, legs would carry them to safety.

Their pursuers had different ideas. Their general had been killed and that had hurt their pride. To hunt and kill the assassins would do much to salve that hurt and so they spread out in a long ragged line that flowed ever upwards even as the sun began its long daytime journey.

Only Georgiou's boyhood memories saved them, for these hills had been his playground and he knew them just thoroughly as Dodd knew the rain-soaked backstreets of his own town. Time and time again he followed the tracks of the goat and the even fainter track left by the rabbit or the hare and so evaded the rush of angry men who called to each other and to the tiny spotter aircraft that sought to see from above what could not be seen from the ground.

Yet it could not last, this game of hide and seek; for two man, no matter how well guided by the ghosts of childhood, cannot long evade the determined efforts of a multitude and Dodd had begun to consider turning at bay and selling his life as dearly as possible when the luck of Papanastasiou came to his aid.

It was the Greek who heard the sound first, stiffening and cocking his head to one side like a foxhound who has heard the bugle call. Matt, listen! Can you hear…'

He never finished the sentence for a sleek, twin-engined fighter roared over the hill, dismissing the spotter aircraft with a brief and disdainful burst of cannon fire. Others followed their leader and soon the valley below them was filled with the sound of gunfire and bomb bursts. There were cries of alarm from their pursuers and the clatter of frightened men retreating down the hillside as the two assassins risked a glance back.

The spotter aircraft was little more than an upright funeral pyre that had set fire to the surrounding bush but the valley below was filled with aircraft that wheeled and dived like so many ferocious gulls and Dodd was reminded of the aircraft he had seen filling the Cretan airfields.

The smaller house that long ago a despairing wife had built was already no more than burning rubble and the defending gun pits were mere charnel houses open to the sky. There was obviously method to this killing and Dodd could only admire the way that the larger house was demolished by bombs and the barracks reduced to fiery splinters.

But still the game was not over; the aircraft not content with demolition became hunters of men and long lines of Greek dust rose in the air as bullets sought homes in flesh until in staggered echelons the aircraft roared back over their heads, their task completed.

Papanastasiou cursed. 'If only we had waited, Matt. We have gone to much trouble for nothing.'

Dodd shook his head. 'No, Lucky. This way we know that Bräuer is dead. It may be that he could have survived. Besides which it was our duty. We couldn't know that attack would take place.'

Lucky shrugged understanding shoulders. 'The bastard's dead and that's all that matters. Perhaps my brother will now lie a little easier, but I do not understand why now, why now when surely Bräuer could have been killed at any time?'

Dodd thought for a moment and was transported back in time to Spain and a rare moment of confession from Comandante O'Neil who had just ensured the death of a German intelligence officer. O'Neil had looked at him with a coldly smiling face and told him that having successfully fed the man a set of lies and half-truths he had decided to have the man assassinated.

'Dead fascists lose the ability to react to a reality I have hidden from them', O' Neil had said and then the moment had vanished with Dodd thankful that such a man was acting on their behalf.

He shook his head at the memory and tried to explain to Lucky that he believed the aircraft had performed the same task only in a less personal and far larger scale. Bräuer had been given a diet of well-fattened lies and had made his dispositions accordingly and was now of no further use to the Allies. Dodd would not be surprised to hear that a series of such attacks were now taking place.

He did his best to explain this and Georgiou grinned his approval.

'This can mean only one thing, Matt. This mean the liberation has begun, for why do it otherwise? You have the bastard's briefcase, which must surely be given to someone who can make sense of it, but before that there is one more task we must do.'

Dodd threw his friend a puzzled look and received a great laugh in return.

'We must seek out your betrothed and my mother for without doubt they will be pleased to see us.' The laugh changed into a smile and a great backslap. 'Come, perhaps you will sample my mother's cooking after all!'

VILLAGE OF THE DEAD

They walked slowly, unwilling foot after unwilling foot.

There was nothing they could do they had seen all they needed to see yet unwilling feet pushed on.

Only heartbreak awaited them, only foretold tales would greet them and yet their feet insisted, one plodding step after another.

High above them a smoke shrouded Greek sun gazed down and a gentle wind held the scents of near dead flame and a dry dust that clung to sweating bodies.

It was a pilgrimage of sorts this journey and a last farewell. There was no agreement to make it only a mutual need that both understood.

There was nothing they could do, they knew this and yet still they walked, the burning smoke giving guidance, telling the tale. The first of the houses appeared now and then another. Tangled timbers and tumbled stones, wisps of smoke and a great silence.

To Matthew Dodd this was an old sight. He had seen burned villages by the hundred in Spain but for Georgiou Papanastasiou the vision brought only anger and great regret.

They walked on, Dodd following his friend as he picked his way through the rubble.

A sudden noise had them reaching for weapons, but they saw only a baleful cat that glared at them, hissing its rage and confusion.

A new smell came to them, a sweet smell though one fearful in its message and both men knew the smell for they had seen battle and death and knew both with intimacy. There was nothing they could do, only bear witness, say last words and shed tears.

It was the body of the priest they saw first. He lay face up, blank eyes staring up to heaven, the wind stirring his beard and his out-flung right hand still held a bible. Georgiou wept great splashing tears, placed the bible on the man's chest and folded his arms over it, the better to protect it and to give the man companionship on his journey to heaven.

The rest of the old men lay a little further on in a small group that lay under the shade of the great tree. They had been childhood friends, grown up together through weddings, births and funerals and now in death they were still joined for they had faced the Germans standing and holding hands.

There was no doubt in Georgiou's mind that they had stood before Saint Peter's wide-open gate and marched through, still together, still holding hands, but there was nothing he could do here on Earth for them but mourn.

Dodd stood in admiration. He had seen courage before and this new sight joined his memory with equality but there was no time to bury, no time other than to kneel before the body of the old grandfather and say farewell.

Tears had streaked the dusty face of Georgiou Papanastasiou but had begun to dry leaving him just as angry and just as lost as the cat. 'May God blight them Matt, may their wives bear bastards, and may they die unshriven. All they know is killing, but look, it seems that God has seen fit to punish their sins.'

He pointed and far up, visible through the haze, were bright white lines cutting through the blue afternoon sky. As they watched one of the lines stuttered and began trailing black clouds which blossomed into a dirty red flower.

'Bombers, Matt, bombers. God is punishing the impious.'

Dodd thought that the bombers had been sent from Crete and not by God, but this did not seem to be the time to be arguing theology.

'It's the invasion, Lucky. The killing of General Bräuer was only the beginning. You saw how full Crete was. Those are heavy bombers. I wonder where they're going.'

Lucky smiled a grim smile. 'They are going to kill Fascists my friend and that is all that matters. I wish them God speed and I wish the same for us. We cannot stay here, my mother and your betrothed wait for us. Let us leave my uncles We have paid our respects and it is time to think of the living. My mother will have set a good pace but men such as us can catch them and surely if the invasion has begun it is best that we bring some good tidings rather than be the bearer of only evil news.'

He glanced around for a last time wiped his face of last tears, muttered a last prayer and then turned to face Dodd. 'Matt, I know where my mother has gone. Many kilometres from here across the hills there is a small valley. In the hot summers when the grass dries and the sheep grow thin this valley stays green for out of the ground flows a small stream which runs for but a short time before returning to the earth. In such times we drive the sheep to the sweet grass and then return leaving our young men to tend to their flocks until God decrees that the rains fall again. The sheep thank us but best of all the valley is very hard to see for a German patrol as the entrance is narrow and guarded by rocks both large and small.'

Together the two men left the village and the old men who had offered up their last years and they took the paths that never ran straight, but always twisted up and curved down. Dodd was utterly lost but Georgiou was on long familiar ground, eagerly pointing out a wayside shrine or a tree climbed in his youth.

Night came and they camped without fire, drank musty water and ate from tins meat of uncertain genealogy. Sleep came to them, each resting while the other stood guard with only the rustle of the wind through the grass to be heard and only kindly stars to be seen.

In the dark black light that heralds dawn they rose and with rested legs marched on, each lost in their thoughts, each wondering just how the villagers would take the loss of so many elderly relatives

They were on the last path now and just as described the path was littered with rocks, some no more than pebbles, others great behemoths that stood pinkly in the first of the dawn.

It was Dodd who first noted the two running figures, the leading figure smaller and running with many a backward glance, the second much larger with longer legs was gaining on the smaller and must soon overtake his prey.

Dodd pulled his companion behind a rock and Georgiou explained that the smaller runner was his nephew, his pursuer unknown. Dodd did not know if the nephew was such by right of birth or marriage or whether it was no more than a courtesy title gained from custom and ease of use but he was growing used to the Greek use of family names to indicate a common community.

Ultimately it did not matter because the panting figure of the nephew ran past them and Georgiou stepped out from behind the rock and drove his fist into the pursuer's stomach.

The second runner turned out to be a rough-clad man in his early twenties with every ounce of breath knocked out of him and close to momentary unconsciousness. He woke to find Georgiou kneeling on him and a long glittering knife pressed against his throat. Dodd stood with the boy while a series of hard questions and harder slaps brought forth reluctant words. Twice he repeated the same words and Dodd could see that Georgiou was making sure the now terrified man was giving up every scrap of information.

At last he relaxed and hope rose in the man's eyes only to die as the long knife was plunged into his throat in a single thrust.

Georgiou rose, avoiding most of the spurting blood and watched weakening hands try to staunch a wound which could never be staunched then spat on the corpse uttering words which even Dodd understood to be curses which would consign the man to an eternity in Hell.

The boy, who was no more than ten had watched the death of his pursuer with a face whiter than any of the surrounding rocks but answered readily enough when questioned in a far gentler tone and at last Georgiou patted the boy on his head and gave words of praise.

'It is as I said, Matt. My mother has led the village to the valley and set a guard at the entrance. Alas they were followed by men who were scouting for a larger group; they have killed the guard and set this scum', he pointed at the blood-soaked corpse, '…in his place. My mother whispered to young Yiannis here that he should run and find what help he could and she chose well for he found us.'

The corpse received a boot which broke unfeeling ribs and another delivery of saliva. 'This scum said that his was a band of communists, but he may have said that as he believed us to be of the same tribe, but it does not matter for we must rescue my people.'

The words were said with a finality which left no doubt that there was only one course of action, and for a moment Dodd thought that his duty must be to deliver a stolen briefcase and let the villagers fend for themselves. But only for a moment. He realised that he had seen too many corpses, too many broken people, broken lives and broken towns, he had not been able to help as but a single man amongst many.

Here he was subject only to his own thoughts and a promise made. He had looked a man in the eyes and promised that for as long as he lived that man's granddaughter would have a strong shield between her and danger and that woman had given him a promise also that come what may she was his. The briefcase was thrust under a rock to be retrieved later if destiny was kind.

Yiannis was given sun-warmed water to drink and then he led the two men to the path that led into a narrow green valley with towering sides that had thrown tumbled rocks onto a stream which ran nimbly between them.

The two men and a boy watched hidden as four men strode up and down shouting out insults to their captives and waving weapons in the air. The women had already been separated from the men. It was obvious that their fate was set. One man had obviously picked his prize. He gestured to Athanasia who shook her head and shrank back while Georgiou's mother stepped forward shouting her objections.

A closed fist put her on the ground and Dodd put a restraining hand on a growling Georgiou.

Athanasia was plucked from the crowd but greeted her captor with raking nails that drew blood and a howl of pain. Her reward was a blow to the head and a reaching hand that ripped the blouse from her body. Angry fire rushed to Dodd's head and shone red light onto thoughts which instantly formed themselves into a plan

'Lucky do you still have your slingshot?'

A puzzled hand pulled out a childhood toy which had already proved deadly.

'Good, now do you see that big chap over by the rock?'

'I see the bastard.'

'Do you think you can hit him?'

Georgiou squinted into the morning sunlight.

'He is very far away, but if I get closer, I can try.'

I need a distraction, Lucky. I need to get in close and I need one of them down before I start.'

Dodd unslung his Sten-gun and began to push his service revolver into the back of his trousers but was stopped by Georgiou who had a tight grin on his face.

'My friend your gun is no doubt a fine weapon, but it is better suited to the killing of tanks, I think. My own pistol is far better for your task, it was a gift from Uncle Sam.' The pistol made an ominous click in his hands. 'Now it is ready. It has killed before so there can be no fear there.'

Dodd unslung his own Sten, recognising as Georgiou already had that such a weapon would kill the innocent as well as the guilty if used. The two Stens and Dodd's pistol were given to Yiannis with instructions to act as a rearguard if the day went ill and then, with a pocket full of pebbles and a hand holding a toy from childhood, Georgiou slipped away using hard-learned warcraft to remain unseen.

Dodd and Yiannis waited and then with a foolish smile fixed to his head Dodd stepped out from behind the rock.

At first the men were puzzled. The man approaching them had no right to be there and yet there he was, wide grin on stubbled face and arms wide open in peaceful supplication. He had no right to be there and despite his friendly greeting he wore a ragged shirt stained with old blood. They called out another challenge, but the grin did not change, nor was the greeting altered. The man continued to walk towards them with an idiot's gait in his legs and an idiot's smile on his lips.

The men were angry, this fool had gone too far and was disturbing what promised to be a pleasant mornings work.

They began to point their weapons.

Dodd's face ached with keeping the smile on his face, his legs measuring a tempo not too fast nor too slow while his arms pleaded to reach behind him and end this pretense.

It could not be, he must be close, closer yet.

They challenged him and he replied using just one of the two phrases Athanasia had taught him. 'Καλημέρα! Good morning!'

He hoped it would be enough, but there could be no turning back now. Another smile, another few steps, another greeting which sounded idiotic even to him.

More steps, a last few.

They began to point their weapons.

The stone had flaws in it. Nature had used Winter's cold hand to break it with icy fingers and the lines stood black against the white. It could not be helped; the stone was the best fit and there was no time to choose again.

He watched the Englishman walk bravely forward towards the confused men, smiling and speaking most of the little Greek that he knew. Despite himself Georgiou grinned, for had Matt decided to use the rest of his Greek then the men would have been truly confused.

'A little further, Matt, just a little further', the words were mumbled and he never knew they were more than thoughts.

There was a last challenge, a last greeting.

They began to point their weapons.

For Matt time both compressed and stretched.

He heard a now familiar whirling and saw the beginning of alarm appear on the men's faces. The whirling rose to a crescendo and then there was the noise of a hundred angry bees and a cry of pain. For a long second's hour every eye was turned and that was enough.

He lost the idiots smile, reached behind him and pulled out a Colt pistol that was one of ten thousand brothers from his waistband, dropped to one knee and sighted the pistol on a man who had only just realised that it was a wolf and not a fool who had entered the valley.

He began to gently squeeze the trigger.

Fast.

Faster.

Round and round with tortured air screaming in complaint.

Childhoods arms now guiding adult intent.

He could see his target taking notice of the strange sound, see a rifle swinging round away from Dodd to where ears told of danger.

A last flick of hand and the stone flew screaming out a challenge.

And missed.

The stone missed, he had aimed at the chest, seeking to break ribs and cripple for a later kill. Lack of skill or some errant breeze caused the stone to lift, flying past the man's head and hitting the boulder behind him where it burst into a thousand shards.

Shards as sharp as any Neolithic axe.

Most missed, venting their spite on the empty air or the uncaring ground but one, just one, flew dagger like, slicing a single eye and flaying open a nose.

In later years, in the company of trusted family and friends Georgiou would shudder at this remembrance and call for laughter to bury the thoughts of what could have happened, but his luck had not deserted him or perhaps it was the soul of a murdered priest whispering in God's ear. Either way, the man dropped his rifle and clapped a hand over an agonized face.

At that moment two shots rang out.

Too late the first man began to turn, lifting a machine pistol that was pointed in almost the right direction.

Almost was not enough and too late was far too late.

Dodd's bullet flung him backwards and the weapon flew from his hands. Without bothering to look further Dodd twisted on his knee, released the trigger and sighted the pistol on a man holding a shotgun. Again, time slowed, again he squeezed the trigger and the man dropped to his knees still holding a shotgun which dying muscles tried to lift and dying fingers tried to fire. For a moment glazing eyes met eyes that had proved to be sure and quick. Then with a last twitch the shotgun discharged its load into the earth and its owner toppled to one side.

Two dead who only moments before were alive, which left one still to kill, but one no longer standing in plain sight.

Dodd had a fleeting glimpse of fleeing legs taking the path which led to Georgiou's nephew and then there was a great booming noise, the legs flew backwards several feet and he knew exactly what had happened. Dodd's revolver wasn't a particularly new design, its bullets were not particularly fast but the gun had long since proven its worth and the bullets were oversized and unsubtle butchers. Somehow Yiannis had found the courage to pick up the revolver and pull the trigger. The pistol was still clutched in his hands, a last wisp of smoke curling up from a cruel barrel while he stared at the flayed body that lay a little distance away.

Because Yiannis was a small boy the bullet had entered through the diaphragm and at an upwards angle.

The lungs were the first to die for such a large bullet was no respecter of important organs. It turned them to pink froth and continued on, tumbling a little as it did so and carving a hole which led to an upper spine which gave way without a fight. Still not content and having lost

136

little of its power at so close a range, it exited the body taking a shoulder blade with it.

The man was dead long before he hit the ground and was no doubt at this very moment explaining to the Devil just how a ten-year-old boy had caused his early arrival in Hell.

Georgiou ran up and took in the scene instantly, the pistol was taken from frozen hands and calming words were poured into ears which still rang from a mighty explosion.

'I have told Yiannis that he has done the right thing, that he has protected his people and that in years to come he can tell of the time when he fought with Mathew Dodd, the lion who fell from the sky to kill the enemy. Matt, my mother, the village waits. We must decide what to do next.'

Dodd followed his friend, passing the body of the man that Georgiou had wounded. Whatever pain he had been in was now over for his head lay crushed under a stone that could only have been lifted by two people. He shrugged. He had seen far worse in Spain and though in better times the man would undoubtably have come to trial in these times the trial had come to him and pronounced sentence of death.

Georgiou's mother was waiting for them with Athanasia at her side, a torn blouse trying and failing to recover its utility. Her eyes met Matt's and there was no shame in them at her near nakedness for there can be no shame when brave mate meets brave mate and she smiled knowing that her grandfather had chosen well.

Dodd then used all that remained of his Greek words and spoke to Athanasia. 'Σ' αγαπώ.' He had been taught them but never truly meant them for how could he mean them on so short a meeting? But he had seen her fight and fight when hope was furthest from her heart and how could he ignore such courage?

There was a truth in the utterance now but no time to act further for the rest of the villagers gathered round and once more argument and counter-argument broke forth in a way that was particularly Greek.

At last it was decided that the dead men would have companions who would undoubtably seek revenge, the village was beyond repair and besides the survivors of General Bräuer's garrison were an unknown and possibly murderous quantity. Therefore, Dodd would lead the entire village towards the Allied army wherever it was.

Dodd was appalled and tried to point out the very real dangers that would result from leading a group of civilians to an area where men were trying to kill each other with deadly skill and advanced technology. In vain he told that it would be far better for scouts to be sent out and bring relief to a valley which could be defended.

His arguments broke on a stubborn Greek wall. Had not Dodd the lion killed a general in single combat, had he not brought the wrath of God upon the garrison, had he not an hour before killed their captors? They were a simple people and had suffered grievous loss but only a fool would fail to see God's hand in all of this.

God had sent Dodd; God had sent a reformed Georgiou and God had in very truth had guided the hands of young Yiannis so that the Devil may take the soul of a bad man. God had done all of this and God would not abandon them now provided that Dodd, with Georgiou at his side, was there to guide them.

In better circumstances, in different circumstances, their faith would have been an embarrassed pleasure and certainly in his eyes an undeserved one, but now that same faith was putting them in danger and worse was putting him in danger and officers of the King had no business putting themselves in danger unless it was in the line of duty and he was not at all sure that the King would see this request as falling into that category.

He was about to refuse as gently as he could when Athanasia stepped forward, her torn blouse fluttering in the morning breeze and her normal smile replaced by a most serious expression.

She stood and spoke simple words. 'Σ' αγαπώ. I love you.'

She knew that if she spoke other words they would be lost, that he would not understand but if she spoke these words he would understand. 'Σ' αγαπώ.'

Dodd heard the words and knew what they meant, not the simple meaning, but the meaning behind the words. 'I trust you, come what may, I trust you. Come what may I will be at your side.'

Love was a great thing but alloyed with trust, love became stronger than the strongest steel and Athanasia had told him that she would never leave his side, that she trusted him to do what was right. He would have to take Athanasia with him and where she went, went the village. It really was that simple and he gave an exasperated smile to Georgiou who burst out into intemperate laughter.

The village would march to the sound of the guns and depend on God's good grace and the luck of a Greek soldier returned to his homeland.

Mathew Dodd had been many things in his life; lawyers' clerk, aide to a general and assassin.

And now it seemed that the fates had given him a new trade…that of shepherd.

GOODBYE SOLDIER

'X-Ray, X-Ray, this is Sun-Burst. Are you receiving me? Over.'

It was hot in the back of the radio truck and Humber Snipes even Humber Snipes adapted to take radio sets were not equipped with many comforts or indeed any comforts at all. The canvas cover did a reasonable job of preventing Greek dust from hurting delicate circuits but it did a far better job of holding in the heat that poured from a hundred glowing valves while failing to hold back the rays of a hot sun.

As a result, Bombardier Milligan and Lieutenant Budden were soaked in sweat and both would probably consider even murder an acceptable price to pay for a cold shower. Alas both knew that the nearest shower was many miles away and it would be days before anyone even thought of providing 19 battery, 56 the Heavy Regiment Royal Artillery with anything like comforts.

'X-Ray, X-Ray, this is Sun-Burst. Are you receiving me? Over.'

The sun shone, the radio crackled its indifference, Milligan sweated and Budden cursed the army, cursed the war and his entire life up to this point. It was the afternoon of their second day in Greece and already the plans drawn up were proving less than robust much to Lieutenant Budden's disgust.

'You'd think we'd have learnt by now; I mean a whole campaign in Spain and by the end of it we knew how to do things, but now? Duck boards and lime, Spike. Where the Hell are they?'

It was a rhetorical question and Spike knew it.

The battery had been provided with the very latest howitzers with far longer range and better accuracy and the gunners declared that they could hit a sixpence placed nine miles away, but the whole regiment had been thrown hurriedly ashore without the many little things which made a working battery an efficient one.

Latrines had been dug, but without lime to kill disease, sickness would soon break out. Duck boards, the great wooden pallets which linked each gun pit were missing also and without them men's feet raised great clouds of dust which evil memory knew brought down the horrid wrath of enemy attention.

Even the water trucks employed to spray dust killing water around the guns were idle because someone had failed to issue orders to fill them. It was, in the immortal words of Gunner Edgington, 'A complete balls up.'

Nevertheless, the regiment had deployed to its appointed place as a small part of the great drive to rescue the parachute regiments who had dropped from the sky in the early hours of the invasion. The hard men who wore the coveted red beret had seized the town and the important cross roads, but like all light troops lacked the tools to defend from those better-armed. Nineteen battery was, with others supposed to ride to the rescue of the beleaguered paratroopers, who would no doubt be suitably impressed and suitably grateful.

However, the ride to glory may very well take place without the comforting power of seven-point two-inch howitzers unless a fickle radio could be returned to fidelity.

'X-Ray, X-Ray, this is Sun-Burst. Are you receiving me? Over.'

The radio only gave crackling laughter and Milligan gave the top of the set a crashing blow from a frustrated fist. Instantly the radio burst into life and Milligan repeated his question but this time with better results.

'Sun-Burst, Sun-Burst this is X-Ray. We are in position and receiving you strength four...Christ, Spike. Where the Hell have you been?' The annoyed voice belonged to Edgington, who along with Lieutenant Goldsmith had been sent up a dry brown hill as shot observers.

A mad gleam came into Milligan's eyes and he gripped the microphone tighter to a grinning mouth. 'X-Ray, X-Ray, this is Sun-Burst. Sorry about the delay. My swonicles needed greasing.'

Milligan had invented a whole new set of words which either had no meaning at all or varying meanings depending on rules which were often made up on the spot. An exasperated lieutenant Budden was told that the use of such words was to frustrate any enemy who might be listening in, but he more than suspected that Milligan's manic behavior was compensating for a deep malaise that was eating up the man from the inside.

The war had swept up Milligan as it had millions of others and most of those others had adapted, some well, others not so well.

Budden looked at the grinning face holding the microphone; Milligan had adapted, but only on the outside; on the inside he suspected that he could hear the screaming of a soul far too empathic for war. There was little he could do about the screaming for though there was a friendship of sorts between them there was also the matter of rank and rank was a barrier that could never be breached. He could only raise an ironical eyebrow at the giggles that came out the speaker.

'In your own time Bombardier, I'm sure the war can wait.'

The words would have crushed a lesser man but Milligan just widened his grin and then transformed himself into a paragon of military efficiency.

'X-Ray, X-Ray, this is Sun-Burst. Are you ready to send co-ordinates, over.'

'Sun-Burst, Sun-Burst, this is X-Ray. Stand by to receive co-ordinates, over.'

Edgington's voice carefully spoke the words and numbers which Milligan wrote down. Then with a nod from Budden he picked up a black tinted phone. 'B sub, require ranging shot, co-ordinates are as follows.

A few hundred yards away tables were consulted and wheels were turned until precisely cut grooves were in agreement and then there was a great roar and the radio truck trembled and deposited back into the air much of the morning's accumulation of dust.

Budden had instantly pressed a stop watch and was counting down the seconds.

Fifty-seven.

Fifty-eight.

Fifty- nine.

Sixty.

Sixty-one.

At sixty-one seconds and somewhere over the hill two hundred pounds of shell moving at eighteen hundred feet per second exploded just a few feet above the ground and both Milligan and Budden looked expectantly at the radio which took only a few moments to bring Edgington's voice back into the truck.

'Sun-Burst, Sun-Burst. This is X-Ray. Corrections as follows…right fifty, drop one hundred, no up, no down.'

Budden grinned. Long practice in Spain had not left them. The battery was as good as it ever was and the irritations of the morning were forgotten in the glow of a job well done.

Milligan gave the corrections and 'B' sub fired for a second time to enthusiastic words from Edgington.

'Right in their lap! You've really pissed on their chips there, Spike! Mr. Goldsmith says that he is ready when you are.'

Spike looked at Budden who gave a delighted grin and then spoke the words that a reluctant radio had delayed.

'Mission battery fire, all subs take station on 'B' sub. Ten rounds independent fire.'

Four guns carefully spaced began speaking in a ragged chorus and far away and out of sight men were caught by a hard rain that shredded flesh from bone and men from life.

19 battery, 56th Heavy Regiment Royal Artillery had fired its first shots in the war to liberate Greece and had every reason to feel proud of itself and all afternoon the guns spoke, men sweated and far away men died as they always do when hot metal meets warm skin.

And all day as men sweated and men died, Greek dust rose and rose.

Rose and rose, as livid a sign as ever men have made.

Up and up from a dry Greek floor to a blue Greek sky.

'Slowly', said Grandfather, 'slowly.

Move slowly, always slowly. Take your time and listen and see.'

Grandfathers voice was soft and his lips barely moved.

'Tell me what you see.'

He looked up at his grandfather with wonder. A face still brown despite the winter but lined with furrows, a woollen hat, green and brown, but most of all the eyes. Grandfather was old past counting, but his eyes were the eyes of a young man. The eyes missed nothing, not even the puzzlement of a grandson.

A soft chuckle escaped old lips.

'You have much to learn boy, much to learn. Now turn, turn slowly like ice and tell me what you see in the glade.'

The glade was no more than bare trees and ice He could see only darkness, light and shadow. There was nothing there but silence.

'Look again boy, look again.'

He looked again, trying to see what grandfather had seen.

There!

There was the tiniest of movement, perhaps the brushing away of a winter fly but now he could see what Grandfather had seen all along.

There in the shade was a magnificent stag, almost invisible again now he had stopped moving.

Grandfather with slow deliberate steps unslung his rifle and chambered a round.

The stag would die for it was a long-established fact that he never missed, never wasted a bullet.

To his surprise Grandfather handed him the rifle.

This was the first time he had held the rifle when it was loaded and he looked up in shock only to receive a silent nod in reply.

He put the rifle up to his shoulder, holding it as he had been taught trying to remember Grandfather's words about wind and elevation.

He put a young eye against the rubber of the little telescope and looked straight into the eyes of the stag. For a moment he thought he saw acceptance there, an acknowledgement that hunter and prey were both separate and yet joined as one.

And then the rifle kicked and the stag fell cleanly, passing from full life into the land of what was.

Grandfather took the rifle and ejected the spent cartridge.

He expected praise or a smile but instead received advice.

'Always kill with reluctance and with sadness, kill for food, kill if you must in defence of family, but never kill with a smile for men who do are cursed.'

The winter scene vanished and he shook his head to clear them of memories, for memories no matter how pleasant could get a man killed out here if taken too far.

There was no snow here, no ice and little in the way of darkened glades. Grandfather had long since killed his last stag and he was a long way from home. Childhood clothes had been discarded and replaced with a smock that mimicked Greek dust and Grandfather's rifle had been replaced by one far more deadly.

The lessons were still with him though, reinforced by months of training. Be still, and be patient, use cover and above all never smile, never lose yourself in the hate for a man who does that is cursed.

He had a task set before him, a simple one for a simple man plucked from the fields that bordered dark woods. Slow the enemy and make them fear. Kill them one by one and never, ever waste a bullet.

Simple orders and ones easy to carry out for a man bred to the farm and the hunt.

When this insanity was over, he would return to the farm and lay flowers on Grandfather's grave and tell the old man how well he had learnt his lessons.

But that was for other days, days when war had been sent back to its bloody cave.

He squinted through the telescope, a tent, a small table, maps, officers who pointed.

Many targets, so many choices.

He had been told that this day would happen; his instructor, a profane little man with the scars of the last war on his face had told him so.

'One day lad you'll have so many targets in front of you, you'll be like a virgin in a whorehouse and you won't know whether to shit or go bust.'

He smiled at the memory. Grandfather would not have approved of the words but the army was not the farm and besides the man was right, he did have too many targets and he did have to choose.

He looked again, the engraved bars on his scope dancing over the group of men.

Choose.

And then the choice was made for him.

The man looked at him.

For a moment he looked into the man's eyes and he thought he saw acceptance there, an acknowledgement that hunter and prey were both separate and yet joined as one.

He squeezed the trigger and the man fell backwards, collapsing the tent on his companions.

The sight was almost comical and but for Grandfather's words he would have smiled.

Still the confusion was his cue to leave and he carefully gathered up his equipment and left using the peculiar shuffling walk that raised as little dust as possible and yet covered ground swiftly.

The day was still young and there were many targets yet to find.

One day, when this insanity was over, he would return and lay flowers on Grandfather's grave and tell him how he had fought for his country.

Fought proudly.

For Germany.

'Cease fire, Spike. It looks like they're retreating, there go our PBI's.'

Edgington's voice was a little ragged after an afternoon's work, but it looked as if in this sector of the battle their work was nearly done; Edgington's laconic last words referred to *Poor bloody infantry,* the words used by even the infantry regiments themselves to describe the army's ultimate argument, the men who must seize ground with rifle and bayonet.

If the infantry was going in then the work of the big guns was over for the infantry had other smaller guns for close support.

Budden gave a sigh of relief.

'Thank Christ for that, sound. Stand down, Spike.'

A dust covered trumpet was picked up and Milligan put it to a dry mouth and instantly cursed as his lips found a grit-covered mouthpiece. Frantic wiping and a brush of mouth produced a simple tune that was repeated three times silencing the guns and bringing relief to aching muscles.

Budden wiped the dust from his tunic and sneezed.

'Bugger!' He sneezed again and made a suggestion that was easy to follow. 'Come on Spike, let's get out of this sweat box.'

It was an easy order to obey and Milligan's hand reached out to end communication with the two men hidden on the far hilltop but before he could say a single word Edgington's voice rattled from the speaker box.

'Spike, Spike, get out! Stukas coming your way! Four of them just passed over us! Spike, do you hear me? Four...'

There was no time to listen, no time to acknowledge only time to react.

Milligan once more put his trumpet to his lips and sounded a strident alarm while Budden, cursing the dust that had drawn down the Stukas ran with Sergeant Fields to the battery's solitary anti-aircraft gun.

Spike looked up and there suspended in the sky were four Stukas, half way into a screaming dive. He had enough time to notice that the aircraft were painted a rather odd brown colour when time stuttered and slowed.

The bombs had been released from the aircraft but seemed oddly reluctant to move further and the Stukas themselves seemed to be moving without hurry. There were red dots on their wing roots and he realised that they were machine guns but he felt no concern, no sense of danger.

He could see a black smoke hovering over the barrel of the Bofors gun and he knew it was firing but it too seemed remarkably still.

Gunner Kidgell stood frozen, a silent Bren gun pointing up.

There was no sound, no noise, no movement...nothing at all.

And then time stuttered again and there was sound and there was noise and there was movement. The Bofors gun barked, the Bren chattered, men shouted and fired rifles at aircraft that were no longer moving with sloth but with malevolent speed. He heard people shouting at him, but he just smiled. He was in no danger, could they not see that?

For some reason it seemed very important to clean the trumpet he still held in his hand and he stood with feet firmly planted on the ground while a grubby handkerchief attempted to bring back a polish the dust had marred

The first of the bombs hit and Spike watched fascinated as 'D' sub gun, seventeen and a half tons of tempered steel was flung round, miraculously staying upright though its camouflage netting, gun laying table and empty shell cases were ripped from the ground and flung far away

Men had dug slit trenches but the Greek soil was hard and full of rocks and men paid with their lives for trenches dug too narrow and in haste.

And then it was over, time regained its tempo and the Stukas droned away like naughty schoolboys who had escaped punishment.

There were screams now and calls for mothers and morphine and Lieutenant Budden ran over and gripped Milligan by the shoulders shaking him like an angry mother shakes a disobedient child.

'What the hell were you doing! You could have been killed there. Don't you know…'

And then there was blood, a lot of blood and a great deal of it was on him and Lieutenant Budden still attempting to hold onto Milligan's shoulders gave out a little gasp and then slumped down onto his knees, his head resting against Milligan's leg as if praying.

Vaguely as if from a great distance he heard Sergeant Field shout, 'Sniper! Get down, get down!'

He heard Gunner Kidgell blaze away with the Bren before another shot rang out and the Bren went silent. He heard all this and yet it seemed unreal. He gazed down on the top of Lieutenant Budden's head and knew the man was dead. He should feel something. The man was his friend and yet try as he might he felt nothing only a great grey nothing where his feelings should be.

That fact should frighten him as well, but again he felt nothing.

Spike Milligan, amateur musician, amateur soldier had been on a journey in this war. The journey had been punctuated by the loss of friends and the burial of a small Spanish child whose loss affected him still. At each tragic point on his journey the road had threatened to rise up and swallow him and only courage and will power had caused him to journey on.

But all journeys must meet a cross roads and Spike Milligan had met his and did not know which way to turn.

And that fact did frighten him.

Goodbye soldier.

THE BATTLEFIELD

They could do nothing for the sheep and Ronnie Prasad could only imagine their panic as they died from an incomprehensible rain.

The huge shells had come down out of the sky and burst overhead into horrid flowers that had flayed the sheep into irregular chunks that even the most amateur of butchers would be ashamed of.

They could do nothing here but make wry jokes and drive on into the next field which had once been a park for trucks. It was more difficult to drive here as this field too had been targeted, but here the shells had been fused for contact and the ground was filled with craters. Every truck had been smashed open and strewn across the dusty grass in a mad jigsaw puzzle and Ronnie knew that he and his crew would find no trade here for massed heavy artillery when used well left little either of flesh or of metal that could mended.

The Germans had attempted to concentrate forces to retake the town that the parachute regiments had taken but alas for them they had been spotted and punishment grim and final had followed.

And so, they drove on to where men had met men and here, they practiced their sad trade, wandering the battlefield that still smelt of blood and cordite. His men spread out joining others whose task was not to mend but to stay Death's hand so that others more skilled might ply their trade on living flesh that had been given every chance. The battlefield, like all battlefields was a sad place, silent in comparison to the fighting that still continued less than a mile away but still it had its sounds. Such as the crackling flames that surrounded a small armoured car that lay on its side the popping sounds as rounds cooked off.

But most of all the cries.

Ronnie hardened his ears to the sounds as long practice had taught him to do; a man who had the strength to cry out was not badly wounded or had given birth to a last burst of adrenaline that must soon be overtaken by death. It was a grim scale that Ronnie measured men by, but it must be so for war had its own logic and would not be denied.

So, Ronnie and his team looked for live men who did not cry out, men who were sliding into shock but could still be saved.

He came across a corporal with the shoulder flashes of a London regiment, a bayonet had pierced his chest and he had lost a lot of blood.

The man gave a weak smile as he saw Ronnie and then died. He saw the light leave the man's eyes for there was a great difference in eyes that saw and eyes which saw no more. The difference could not be described but Ronnie knew it when he saw it.

There was no need to check for a pulse, the man was dead and beyond any help that he could give.

He uttered a short prayer asking the Gods to look kindly upon the soul in its next reincarnation and moved on to a large hole that could only have been caused by a heavy mortar.

Most of the mortar's victims were bloody lumps, but one man must have been at the very edge of the blast circle and still lived.

Ronnie moved quickly and ran practiced hands over the man. A broken leg with the bone just piercing the flesh, a mangled left hand and a torn stomach. The man was just entering the first stages of shock with a light sheen of sweat on a pale face so he would have to move quickly. A quick pull on the leg brought a sharp cry of pain, but now there was less chance of a sharp-edged bone severing a blood vessel. The blood which pulsed from the hand was stopped with a tourniquet which left only the stomach which had been sliced open revealing several coils of gut which now lay on the man's stomach.

Throughout all this the man had not spoken a single word and Ronnie wondered if this was another sign of shock and worked all the harder, but now the man spoke.

'Könnte ich bitte etwas Wasser bekommen?'

The words were unfamilar but one stood out and made the meaning clear.

Ronnie knew that stomach wounds induced a terrible thirst, he also knew that giving the man even a spoonful of water would be the very worst thing he could do, but the man had asked so politely he was almost shocked into breaking one of the laws of combat medicine, instead he put on a reassuring smile and replied a gently as possible.

'I'm sorry mate, that would just bugger you up worse, now hold still because this is going to hurt a lot.'

He made no attempt to reinsert the coils of gut. For all he knew the man's stomach was full of shrapnel and poking around blindly would only make things worse. Instead he placed a thick pad of gauze over the wound and began to wrap a bandage around the man lifting him up as gently as he could though despite his care the man groaned and a trickle of blood flowed from a bitten lip.

'I'm sorry mate, but we're nearly done.'

He hoped the man understood, but his tone was soothing and that was the best he could do. He rummaged around in the man's pack, pulled out a waterproof cape and placed it over the man. A body going into shock lost heat like a runaway sun and insulating the skin and trapping heat was almost as important as slowing blood loss.

There was time now to do other things, the man would not die…at least not yet, and it was time to prepare him for his journey.

A water bottle soaked a length of gauze which was pressed to the man's lips and Ronnie pulled out a vial of morphine from his kit bag and waved it before the man's eyes.

'Nict pain…verstayan?'

Ronnie spoke English, Hindi and Maori, but his German was far from perfect. The man seemed to understand and sighed with relief when the vial was emptied into his skin.

He had done all he could and signaled for stretcher bearers, tearing off a pad of paper on which he wrote all that he had seen and done and thrust it into the pocket of the man's tunic.

The stretcher bearers applied a bag of fluids, splinted the leg and then carried away the wounded man. Ronnie would never see the man again, would never know if he lived or died.

He didn't have time to worry though, for the battlefield was overfull and time marched in lock step with mortality to remove men from life before the overworked medics could reach them.

It was an exhausted Ronnie Prasad who drove back to the field dressing station that late evening, ate a hasty meal and collapsed fully-clothed onto a camp bed and dreamt of Italian dogs, gunfire and gods.

He woke next morning to find himself directed to the Captain's tent and he wondered what sin of omission or commission he had performed to warrant such a summons, but Captain McKinney was smiling when he reported in.

'Think of it as a sort of busman's holiday, Prasad. All you have to do is drive there, pick the chap up and bring him back here and let us have a look at him.'

And so, Prasad, in the company jeep, negotiated harassed military policemen and the long lines of traffic which was making heavy weather of roads which insisted on being unable to decide exactly which direction they preferred and it was midday when he pulled up outside the headquarters of the 56th Heavy Regiment, Royal Artillery.

He had not even switched off the engine when the tent flap was violently thrust aside and a red-faced major leapt out, looked over at Prasad and without saying a single word in greeting screamed at the top of his voice. 'Sergeant, bring out the prisoner!'

A broad-shouldered Sergeant appeared along with a thin man with one of the palest, saddest looking faces Prasad had ever seen.

The major put his face up to the face of the sad man and proceeded to bellow in his face. 'Do you see who they've sent for you, Milligan? A wog! That's what they think of you, and that's what I think of you as well! You're finished, Milligan, finished!'

The man was almost spitting his fury and then with a few curt words to the Sergeant strode off leaving the thin man shaking with fear.

Having watched the major disappear from sight the sergeant returned to the tent and brought out a canvas chair into which he pushed the unprotesting, thin man and then thrust out a hand for Prasad to shake.

'I'm Sergeant Eccles, can I have word…private like, just Sergeant to Sergeant?' He paused and looked around to see if he could be overheard. 'That was Major Jenkins and he is, not to put too fine a point on it a cunt of the first order.'

He looked at Prasad's medal ribbons. 'Greece the first time and a M.i.D?'

'And Gibraltar as well', agreed Prasad.

Eccles nodded. 'Well with us it was Spain and it was a fuckin' nightmare. Women as could shoot the eye out of a man at five hundred feet and kids that ad soon as knife a sentry as play with a toy. We saw some sights I can tell you and young Spike there 'e saw 'em too…and

152

worse. Well 'e put a brave face on it, same as all of us, but it stayed with him worse than most I reckon.

'Yesterday 'is battery got stonked good an' proper by Stukas and then they lost an officer and couple of other ranks and that was it for poor Spike; 'e broke an' no mistake. Cries 'e does and shakes fit to wake the dead.

Eccles dropped his voice at little as if divulging a great secret.

'Thing is, the major fancies himself as a bit of a trumpet player and 'e ain't but 'e don't think that, and 'e challenged Spike to a contest while we were on the boat coming over. Course Spike pretty much blew his balls off and the major 'as never forgiven him so there's bad blood between them and as soon as the major heard about Spike 'e drags 'im up 'ere, strips him of 'is rank and tears into 'im something' fierce. Wants to send 'im up for court martial 'e does, some bollocks about disobeying orders in the face of the enemy.'

Eccles grinned, showing glee and missing teeth.

'Only 'e can't 'cos army regulations says that there has to be a medical examination first, which is why you are here. So, wot I want to say is that the lad ain't a bad lad and better than most. All 'e needs is a bit of a rest and 'e will be back on his feet in no time at all.'

There was a pause and Eccles's hand was thrust out again. 'Sorry about that *wog* thing. Spike won't mind, grew up in India 'e did.'

There was a little confusion on Eccles's face as he read Prasad's shoulder flashes which made no mention of India.

'It's a long story', said Prasad grinning and liking the Cockney sergeant immensely. The man had gone out of his way to help a comrade and that raised him in Prasad's eyes. 'Perhaps another day if we meet again.'

The missing teeth showed themselves again and handed over a folder with the warning that Prasad was not to believe a word of it, but was to remember everything which had been said.

Ronnie walked over to the thin man and asked him to move into the jeep and received only a blank look in reply. Resigning himself to the inevitable he pulled the man he now knew as Gunner Milligan to his feet and deposited him into the passenger seat of the jeep. 'My name is Sergeant Prasad. I'm part of the New Zealand Medical Corps. I'm here to take you to a place where you can be looked after. Do you understand?'

There was no reply…only a jelly-like body and unfocused eyes. Ronnie sighed with frustration and compassion and then thought of something Sergeant Eccles had said and so repeated his questions in Hindi.

To his surprise and relief, he got a reply in the same language. It wasn't much of a reply as the man in his present state could not be expected to hold a conversation, but it was a start and the journey back was conducted with Prasad conversing in Hindi and receiving one word answers in the same language until the early evening brought Prasad back to where he started.

Captain McKinney was Scot by birth who had received a first class medical degree from a first class Scottish university, but almost before the ink had dried on his sheepskin he took a third class cabin on the first boat he could find that was leaving for New Zealand where he fitted in very well having a no-nonsense disposition coupled with a healthy disdain for authority and rules.

Ronnie knew that he ran a good organisation where everyone was left alone to do their jobs in peace but the man who sat alongside him was obviously terrified of the captain for he shook uncontrollably.

He explained to McKinney just what Sergeant Eccles had told him and the fact that the man would only converse in Hindi.

'Reminds him of a safer time I shouldn't wonder. I need to ask him a few questions…if you wouldn't mind, Sergeant?

Ronnie turned to the still trembling Milligan and spoke as gently as he could in the Hindi still used by his family. 'This man means you no harm. I swear by the holy book that this is the truth. This man bears to you only good will and will not betray you.'

To no one's surprise Milligan burst into tears and the gentle questioning began.

Later when the trembling gunner had been given a large sleeping tablet and poured into a bunk bed McKinney and Prasad met again under a wine dark sky with the distant sounds of battle in their ears.

'Well what do you think?' McKinney's voice was not a soft one by nature, but he spoke quietly not as captain to sergeant but as colleague to colleague.

Prasad shrugged, 'I think we send him to a psych unit and let them deal with him. We don't have the tools.'

He paused and both men watched the horizon glow for a moment until the darkness returned once more. 'And we certainly don't have the time…and you know it.'

McKinney nodded for all that had been said was true and yet there was something about the case that disturbed him. 'He says he doesn't want to go, Ronnie. He says he knows he can't go back to his unit but he wants to feel useful.' He didn't strike me as a malingerer. If we send him back, God alone knows where he'll end up.'

Ronnie raised a disagreeing eyebrow. 'So? We're combat medics. I bring them in, you sew them up, then we pack up camp, move on and hope there isn't a bullet out there with our name on it. He's a radio operator, we've already got one of those and what else can he do?'

Now it was McKinney's turn to shrug 'So, what do we do, Ronnie? Send him into the system and hope he can find a psychiatrist that speaks Hindi? You know what will happen to him, they'll pump him full of drugs and lock him away. You can help him Ronnie, you know you can.'

'All 'e needs is a bit of a rest and 'e will be back on his feet in no time at all.' Sergeant Eccles voice came back to Ronnie like an uncomfortable dream and he thought about the strict injunction Hinduism taught about not causing pain to others being the sum of all other duties.

There were black shadows infesting Milligan's soul, that much was plain and there was his own soul to think about. Would rejecting this chance to heal a man hurt his chances of bettering his own soul? He was a healer that was plain also, a little rough but always ready. But was he ready for this?

McKinney watched the emotions playing on Prasad's face and wondered if it was fair doing this to a good man but the alternative was condemning a man to a living death in an institution.

There was a great sigh from Prasad.

'How long?'

'A month.'

'Two weeks.'

Split the difference, Ronnie, call it three.'

'No combat duties though, he couldn't take it, besides which he might get me killed.'

'A good point I'll have you transferred to the Canadian field hospital, and three weeks, I promise. If he's not on the mend by then, I'll ship him out myself and, in the meantime, it would be best if his paperwork becomes lost…and Ronnie?'

'Yes?'

'Thank you.'

There was no reply from Ronnie Prasad for the man was thinking of home where the smells were different, the light less white, the hills gentler and birds sang sweeter songs.

He was a long way from home and now he had a companion where none was sought, a companion who might very well prove a great liability.

There was nothing he could do now but pray to the Gods.

And hope.

THE FIELD HOSPITAL

The twenty-fourth Canadian Medical Corps field hospital was filled with the scents of sweating men, fresh cut pine and the creaks of stiff canvas being pulled into useful shapes. It was a chaotic scene and Ronnie Prasad wandered through groups of busy men and people far too hurried to spare either him or his silent companion a second glance.

The hospital had moved to follow the fighting and was doing so to a rigid schedule that left no time at all for strangers and it was a long journey before he arrived at his destination.

The Canadian nursing sister did not look at all like one dedicated to easing the suffering of wounded men. Instead she looked like a mechanic, complete right down to the hammer which was held firmly by the end of its handle just as every good mechanic should.

She wasn't dressed like a nurse either; the starched headdress had been replaced by a torn woollen hat and the pristine white uniform had been exchanged for stained battle dress that fell over khaki trousers held up by a wide black belt.

Prasad was not at all sure that that he was about to talk to the right person but a harassed doctor had pointed to her and he was left with little choice.

'Excuse me ma'am, I'm sergeant Prasad and I've been ordered to report here.'

He thrust out his orders and wondered just what the correct military protocol was for reporting to a female officer of another nation who was not in uniform or at least not in any generally recognised uniform that he had ever seen. It didn't seem to matter though as the woman thrust the hammer into an overstretched pocket and took the orders, reading carefully through them and glancing first at Prasad and then at Milligan who stood forlornly some distance away.

She muttered something under her breath in French and then spoke in an English which had undertones of Quebec. 'You think that I will give three weeks here enjoying peace and quiet while you and your friend amble about and you attempt a little amateur psychiatry? I know your captain; he's a good surgeon and his heart is in the right place, but three weeks, Sergeant? I do not think so.' The hammer was pulled from her pocket and pointed at Prasad's chest. 'This is a working hospital and you pair are going to work and work very hard indeed.' There was a dangerous glint in her eyes and an even more dangerous smile on her face as she spoke and Prasad 's heart sank just a little.

He turned to see if his silent companion had understood the nurse's words. There was still an unusual expression on Milligan's face that was a mixture of apathy, hope and fear.

It was his job to vanquish Milligan's demons leaving only the hope but just how the third son of a farmer from New Zealand was supposed to accomplish that task had not been explained to him.

He spoke a few words in Hindi designed to give comfort and the hope in Milligan's eyes grew…but only a little.

It was going to be a long three weeks and the woman's grin gave no comfort at all.

War was Hell on Earth and it was the nature of Hell that its suffering fell not just on those who wore a uniform but on those who did not and had the least understanding of its dangers.

The girl was perhaps four years old with bright blonde hair that fell in tresses over a face dirtied by tears and drawn tight with pain. Her father stood by her side with his own tears running down his face while Ronnie looked at a hand that was red and blistered.

He had seen such burns before; smoke grenades occasionally failed to go off but a little incautious play could overcome their reluctance with the resulting coloured smoke causing much childish glee. Alas such joy came at a price, for after discharge the canister remained far more than merely warm as the girl had found to her cost.

Spike Milligan applied a liberal dose of Vaseline and Ronnie wrapped the tiny hand in gauze explaining with signs and gestures the care that the father should give in the days to come. The father's reply was in Greek but it was not hard to guess its meaning and Ronnie nodded absent-mindedly and waved the next patient forward.

This was the end of the first week of Ronnie and Spike's exile.

They had been given a small and ill-used ambulance equipped with supplies, a temperamental radio and a map and told to minister to the civilian population of Greece who had suffered even as they were liberated for an army had rolled across this land leaving scars that would take the work of many seasons to remove and as armies have ever done it had left destruction in its wake.

Ronnie's battered ambulance was a very small part of a very large effort to return to Greece some stability and sense of order. He didn't know this and had no need to know this; all he had was days where he followed the still fresh tank tracks and nights where he tried to talk to a still reticent Spike. He spoke of a home far away, a small farm, of rolling hills that faced a pure blue sea, of the bellbirds that sang sweet songs from swaying tree ferns and of a family that looked both inwards and outwards. He talked of his soul and this body in which it had taken temporary shelter and the duty he owed to it and the duty he owed to others.

His words lured Spike into conversation, not only for his patient's sake but for his own as he was genuinely interested in how Spike saw the world for Hinduism is a belief which sees a thousand paths to enlightenment and progress. As ever the conversation was in Hindi, but he noticed that each night the conversation became a little longer, a little more enthusiastic

This was undoubtably a good thing but the pages of the calendar were rolling ever forward and a Spike Milligan who still needed drugs to sleep, still spoke mostly Hindi and who started like a nervous colt at every sudden noise was a Spike Milligan who was going to be locked away in a psychiatric ward no matter what Ronnie thought or wanted.

He did his best, keeping away from the path of armoured thrusts and dealing with the mundane and the accidental by day and conversing over cold meals by night.

Night after night he talked of the old gods and semi mythical kings and emperors who taught lessons on behavior and how to seek the paths of duty and kindness that led to the fulfilment and enlightenment that was the desire of every Hindu.

Night after night he did this, always seeking and never truly finding a key to change the shape of Milligan's heart.

And yet night after night, long after Spike had entered a drug induced sleep, he lay awake and wondered why he had never told his companion about the dog.

The dog was real; months ago in distant Gibraltar he had crouched on the edge of a shell crater while a half-captured Italian engineer stood and held clamps and a bright light so that two men could be saved where without help only one might live.

The dog had brought the engineer to him and that was a miracle of its own but once its task was complete it sat with infinite patience and lolling tongue. He could spare little in the way of glances towards the dog for spurting arteries and failing lungs took every effort. Later though, after he was sure that both men had been given every chance he walked with the dog and its owner in a last farewell before both walked through the gates of captivity.

It was then that the dog looked at him and grinned.

There was old wisdom in the eyes and the grin was definitely a grin and not some random canine twitch.

Ronnie Prasad was a practical man for life had made him so, but he knew, as every sensible man knew that the gods moved about the Earth in disguise hiding their true form the better to perform their tasks.

Ronnie had been visited by a god, of that much he was certain and that would have been blessing and contentment enough but for his dreams.

In his dreams the dog came to him and talked, sometimes the dog spoke in Hindi, sometimes in English or in Maori but whatever language the dog used, when morning light broke sleep's grip Ronnie could not remember a single word nor recall a single drop of imparted wisdom.

His blessing had turned into curse and perhaps that was why he never revealed the presence of the dog, for what would be the use of speaking of bad dreams to a man whose whole life had turned into walking nightmare?

And so the first week died and gave birth to the second.

Sometimes the radio spoke and gave them directions to a supply dump or a village of no particular significance, sometimes the radio remained silent, but always there were the high hills with green flanks and the mountains behind them that were so high only the bravest of clouds clung to them. And the people, always there were the people who trusted the two men with fever-ridden children or old bones that had worked too hard.

But every act of healing rubbed away a little of the stone of time and the second week ran to its death on swift feet while Prasad drove and drove. It was a rare night that was spent under a caring roof and the worn-out ambulance travelled along roads that were never straight and over hills that were far too steep for the plough.

The high tide mark was reached now and a weary Prasad turned the wheel back to a temporary home feeling shame and frustration over a duty unfulfilled, for what use was a healer that could not heal?

A childhood's teaching taught that duty must be ever be done lest the soul shrink and regress and still his companion insisted on using the words learnt in a safer world, a world not ruled by the bullet or the Stuka. Yet he was as the gods made him and his soul retained a flicker of optimistic flame within it and as a dying sun flared gold light on black Greek hills, he told himself that there was still time if the gods willed him another miracle.

The troubled snores of Spike Milligan reminded him that sleep beckoned and he allowed himself to seek an earned rest and close weary eyes. The sun followed his example and blackness crept with stealthy fingers over the ambulance, a frustrated healer, and a man who had fought against the demons of war with tools all too poor. Spike's dreams were few for a white tablet of calm had been taken and Morpheus held him in an iron grip.

But Ronnie Prasad had no such help and Morpheus took him on a different journey.

A far different journey.

He could feel a gentle wind on his face, smell the scents of new-mown hay and thyme. He looked down at brown arms thrust out from rolled sleeves which had begun to sweat a little for the sun was hot. In the distance was a mountain range still wearing the threadbare cap of last winter's snow and in front of him a steep-sided hill that had grown a tumbling stream which ran with joyous sound to a building of piled stone and shingled roof.

He was standing on a narrow path built of full-baked bricks that led arrow straight past the building and up to the mountains beyond. A golden light was rolling down the path fading as it got nearer and forming itself into the shape of the dog.

'Here is the path', the dog said. 'Will you take it?'

Ronnie pulled all his courage into a quivering lump and spoke. 'Are there other paths?'

The dog grinned and raised an airy paw.

'There are always other paths but this one leads to your heart's desire, so I ask again…will you take this path?'

The quivering lump hardened as Ronnie saw that there could be but one answer. 'I will take the path.'

The dog's grin widened and a golden tail wagged with pleasure.

'Good! The path is steep and there is a toll to pay, but I will wait for you and guide your steps.'

The dog vanished and Ronnie was left standing on the path while the mountains faded from view, the happy stream gurgled into silence and even the wind died against his cheek.

He woke with a contented smile on his face and a body full rested. He had not dreamt, of that much he was certain. Dreams were no more than the twitchings of a sleeping mind disturbed by the thunder of war and what he had experienced was far more than that.

He laid a gentle hand on Spike's shoulder breaking him from a drug-induced sleep and the two men began the daily rituals common to all men in all wars and soon a tired engine was pulling them along a half-beaten track.

Ronnie's smile never left his lips as he drove to the next mountain village, he had no idea what awaited him only that he was on a sure path.

And that was what mattered most.

FICTION FROM APS BOOKS
(www.andrewsparke.com)

AJ Woolfenden: *Mystique: A Bitten Past*
Davey J Ashfield: *Footsteps On The Teign*
Davey J Ashfield *Contracting With The Devil*
Davey J Ashfield: *A Turkey And One More Easter Egg*
Fenella Bass: *Hornbeams*
HR Beasley: *Nothing Left To Hide*
Lee Benson: *So You Want To Own An Art Gallery*
Lee Benson: *Where's Your Art gallery Now?*
Lee Benson: *Now You're The Artist…Deal With It*
Lee Benson: *No Naked Walls*
TF Byrne *Damage Limitation*
Nargis Darby: *A Different Shade Of Love*
J.W.Darcy: *Ladybird Ladybird*
Jean Harvey: *Pandemic*
Michel Henri: *Mister Penny Whistle*
Michel Henri: *The Death Of The Duchess Of Grasmere*
Michel Henri: *Abducted By Faerie*
Amber J Hughes: *An Injection Of The Unexpected*
Hugh Lupus *An Extra Knot*
Ian Meacheam: *An Inspector Called*
Ian Meacheam: *Time And The Consequences*
Tony Rowland: *Traitor Lodger German Spy*
Andrew Sparke: *Abuse Cocaine & Soft Furnishings*
Andrew Sparke: *Copper Trance & Motorways*
Phil Thompson: *Momentary Lapses In Concentration*
Paul C. Walsh: *A Place Between The Mountains*
Paul C. Walsh: *Hallowed Turf*
Michael White: *Life Unfinished*

Printed in Great Britain
by Amazon